FLINT

INTERGALACTIC DATING AGENCY

DRAGON BRIDES
BOOK NINE

KATE RUDOLPH

ABOUT FLINT

Dragon lord Flint's hunger for excitement leads him to Intergalactic Dating Agency: Adventures who promise to find him a mate who matches his own fiery desires.

Human Liza has no idea aliens exist - or that she's been talking to an alien dating agency for months, pouring her hear out about her abusive home life. When she finally begs for help, Flint's right there... but she has no idea why. And when he teleports her away from home she's sure she's being abducted.

In her desperate bid to escape, Liza sends them hurtling down to a dangerous watery planet full of monsters eager to eat her... or worse. Liza refuses to rely on any man, even if her accidental kidnapper is a better option than a wild water dragon. But as she and Flint are thrown closer together, sparks and flames fly amidst the chaos. Soon Liza's questioning whether she wants to go home again.

Maybe abduction isn't such a bad thing, after all.

1

Erica's side of the bedroom looked like a bomb had gone off. Even a month after her sister's escape, the place was a mess. And Liza was starting to admit to herself that Erica wasn't coming back. She had her boyfriend, Troy, now. She was safe.

Downstairs, the door slammed, and Liza flinched. Her dad was home. But maybe he wouldn't realize that she was. She kept folding the clothes that Erica had left behind, moving around on light feet. The floorboards had an annoying habit of creaking, betraying her to her father's anger at night when she was supposed to be asleep. But it was three PM. Not even the most irrational man could think she'd gone to bed.

There was something hard in the pocket of an old pair of Erica's jeans. Liza reached in, and her fingers brushed against cool metal. She pulled it out, and her heart twisted. The cheap silver bracelet didn't look like much. The clasp was tarnished, and one of the charms had already fallen off.

Liza had scrimped and saved to afford the thing for Erica's sixteenth birthday. Her sister loved shiny things. She'd found a piece of obsidian rock somewhere and kept it on her nightstand like a talisman since they were children.

The rock was gone. The bracelet was here. Erica didn't care enough to take it when she moved out.

Liza's fist curled around the cheap metal, threatening to bend the edges of the charm, and she squeezed her eyes shut before they could do something stupid like start to tear up. It was a cheap bracelet. So what if Erica had forgotten about it?

All of Liza's life, she'd been determined to keep her little sister safe. And now she was. For some value of safe. Troy wasn't the kind of guy Liza would have wished for her sister. He worked at the factory with their dad. He liked going to the bar. And she had seen a sly grin on his face more than once before he and Erica started dating.

But she hadn't tried to stop Erica from leaving. Not when it meant escaping this house.

"Liza! Get your ass down here now!" The thunderous roar of her father's voice made her freeze in place. Liza set the bracelet down on the side table and took three seconds and two deep breaths before hurrying down the stairs.

Dad didn't sound drunk, and she wasn't sure if that was a good or bad thing. He'd been drinking more lately. Coming in at all hours, driving down the roads and putting everyone's life in danger. But when he was at the bar, he wasn't home, and that made him someone else's problem.

Her father stood in the kitchen, a dangerous look on his face. "How dare you leave this mess in here! I keep a roof over your head. I expect a little respect." He jammed his finger at the countertop, and Liza's heart sank.

She hadn't noticed the ring on the counter from her coffee mug earlier. She was usually better than that, but she'd been distracted by something stupid. Some stupid dream that wasn't going to get her anything.

"And what about this mess in the sink?" He nodded toward the basin.

There were two dishes. Both of them from her father's breakfast. Why was she so damn stupid? She knew he got like this. It didn't take anything to set him off, and it was easy as hell to load the dishwasher.

Liza lowered her gaze and felt her shoulders slump. "I'm sorry, sir. I'll do it right now." Her father stalked away, making an angry sound in the back of his throat. He didn't touch her. He didn't hit. He wasn't that mean. But sometimes he got too close. Sometimes he held on to her arm a little too long, his grip a little too tight. Rarely did he leave bruises. She knew he could.

She had to get out of here.

It only took two minutes to tidy up the kitchen, and as she went to throw away a used paper towel, her eyes snagged on something in the wastebasket.

The job fair.

She snatched the flyer out of the trash and wiped off some of the coffee grounds that were starting to stain it. Luckily, none of those landed on the floor, where there would be hell to pay.

Harper Forest Valley Job Fair. Saturday, 1:00 PM to 4:00 PM. Entry-level positions available. Walk in and get hired.

She wasn't stupid. The kind of jobs they were offering there weren't going to pay much. But she didn't need much. Rent in the Valley wasn't too bad. She just needed out of this house.

And she wasn't going to depend on some guy like Troy—or her father—to give her a new home.

She'd grabbed the flyer on a whim while she was out picking up groceries last week. Her dad didn't want her working. Why let his daughter work when he could have a maid at home?

But Erica was gone.

Liza could finally get out. All she had to do was go on Saturday. All she had to find was a place that would be happy to hire a twenty-four-year-old with no work history and nothing more than a high school education. Easy.

Right?

It would be okay. She could make it work.

Her father stepped back into the room, and she didn't hide the flyer fast enough.

"You're going to start paying rent next month," he snarled at her, finger pointed like a weapon. "You don't pay a cent, you don't clean up, and I've been feeding you for free for too long. You have to start carrying your own weight. One thousand bucks on the first of the month. You pay me, or you get the hell out." He didn't give her time to respond.

A thousand bucks? Liza didn't have two quarters to rub together, let alone hundred-dollar bills. The first of the month was less than a week away.

Tears threatened again, and she crumpled up the job fair flyer. She tossed it in the trash and went back up to her room, imagining all the ways her dad could rot in hell.

Her phone sat on the bedside table, the notification light blinking invitingly. She picked it up, hoping it was some funny video or cute puppy but was even happier to see that it was a message from IDA.

She wasn't exactly sure what IDA was. Some sort of service for people like her, with shitty dads and no way out. She'd been chatting back and forth with the bot, or possibly the volunteer, or whoever was on the other side of the line, ever since two days after Erica left.

Right then, with her father's demand ringing in her ears and the certainty that she was never going to actually get out of this place, she poured her heart out into her message.

"I wish I could be anywhere but here right now. I wish somebody would take me away."

She wasn't going to let any dude from this town rescue her, but some distant part of her brain, something that still nurtured fantasies that she was far too old to dream about, wished there was a hero out there somewhere, some fantastical guy who could ride in on a white horse and take her off to his castle.

She huffed out a hollow laugh and tossed the phone aside. Erica's room was still a mess. The cheap bracelet glinted in the room's light, a reminder of things that could be left behind.

Saturday, Liza would find a job. She'd find a place to sleep that wasn't her father's house. Because she wasn't giving that man one damn cent. But for just another few minutes, she let herself dream.

———

The controls rattled under Flint's hands, and he cursed whoever had designed this ship. What was wrong with a simple joystick? He had buttons and scroll wheels and more than one shaft he wasn't sure what to do with.

Should he have stayed for the training that was offered when he purchased his new baby? Maybe.

But Flint wanted open space. He needed the feel of freedom that came when there was no one within one hundred light years. Or at least when it felt that way.

He was regretting that freedom now as his ship

rocked and dodged through one of the thickest asteroid fields he had ever encountered. Had someone blown up a planet? Where had all the debris come from?

His ship's defensive field was doing its job— more or less—but it made for a rocky ride. Then the proximity alert blared over the speakers, the whole display in front of him going red in warning. Flint cursed and pressed what he thought was the emergency evasive maneuvers button. It was big and red, and he couldn't miss it.

Reality warped around him, and the view screen resolved into a planet's surface, a giant bubbling volcano in front of him. Not the invasive maneuvers button. Shit!

Who would put the teleport button right there?

Flint slammed on it again, and reality warped once more, landing him safely at the edge of the asteroid field as if he'd never been in danger.

He slumped back in his chair, letting out a relieved sort of laugh and petted the edge of the dashboard, careful not to hit any of the buttons or other controls.

He'd review the control footage later, but right now that felt like a close call, closer than it had in quite some time.

Knox would kill him when he learned about this. If Knox bothered to call anymore. Flint was being uncharitable towards his brother. Towards Asher too.

Both of his fellow triplets had recently found their mates. They were happier than he'd ever seen them. Well, Asher being happy at all was a new circumstance altogether. His brother had needed to loosen up for more than a decade. That mate of his head finally got him to see that.

Knox though ... He and Flint had been close. Knox was the one Flint told about his close calls. He endured his brother's warning glares and laughed off his brushes with death. Would Knox even answer if he gave him a call right now?

Flint wouldn't do it anyway. He always saved his reports of near-death experiences and derring-do for when he flew home. He didn't need to worry anyone unnecessarily. And he wasn't going to pull anyone away from their mate.

Flint set a course he knew would be safe, not that he was heading anywhere specific. He had friends in half a dozen systems he could call on. He could head home, shift into his dragon form, and fly through the mountains for a month to get his head on right.

Or he could just sit here alone and wallow in his loneliness.

Flint groaned. Maybe there was something to that thing his brothers had done.

The Intergalactic Dating Agency.

The Royal Matchmaker.

He would never have considered it before. He was happy in his adventurous single life. Women on every planet. Adventures wherever he chose to find them. New spaceships with shoddy controls. He could have everything.

But maybe it was time for something else. He wasn't ready to settle down and hang up all of his adventuring gear just yet. But the Intergalactic Dating Agency had a solution for that. IDA Adventures. It was for people who didn't just want their match delivered to them. For people who wanted a bit of intrigue. A bit of an escapade.

For people exactly like Flint. He logged into his account and saw he had a message waiting. Not just a message. A mission. The agency had matched him with a woman on Earth, a human, desperate to get out of her situation. She was begging for rescue, wanted someone to sweep her away.

He could do that. He didn't know if she was his mate or someone he might have a bit of fun with for a while before they parted ways, hopefully as friends. He didn't like to leave anguished lovers behind. Not that he could remember anyone caring enough about him to be particularly anguished when he moved on to the next planet.

He changed his course with the setting for Earth. It was an out-of-the-way planet, one rarely visited by aliens, though it could be prime pickings for slavers looking to fill up their holds. Earth didn't have planetary defenses. It didn't know it needed them. It also didn't know that it was in the shadow of the Imperium. One day that empire would sweep in and claim it for its own. It could be a century away. Perhaps two. Nothing to worry about today.

Flint would have to go in stealthily. He used his brand-new teleporting feature to cross the galaxy in a matter of hours rather than months. But once he was in the correct system, he had to wait for night-fall. His ship had stealth mode, but it wasn't invisible. And while Earth wasn't aware of aliens, they did have defensive systems for threats from their own planet.

He wasn't about to let himself get shot down so far from home. He would never hear the end of it.

If he survived.

As the hour struck, he broke through the

atmosphere and flew to the right coordinates. He wasn't sure how he was supposed to do this. Break into her dwelling and steal her from her bed? Did she know that he was coming today? Was she already waiting for him with a backpack? Would someone try and stop them?

Anticipation swelled in his veins as he scanned the environment with his ship's delicate controls. They were in a mountainous, heavily forested region with narrow roads and dwellings that were miles apart. What if he grabbed the wrong woman?

He huffed out a laugh. Wouldn't that be something? Come all this way and accidentally rescue the wrong woman. Someone would know about aliens then. But he had an image of her from the IDA, and his ship's scanners were sensitive.

As he hovered just above the tree line with his stealth mode activated, his ship pinged a warning of movement behind his match's house. A dark-haired woman carrying a bulging white bag slipped out the back door and walked to the outbuilding that had three large green bins in front of it. She placed the bulging bag in one of the bins and turned to return to the house. But before she made it halfway, she paused and looked up.

Right at his ship.

There was no sign of recognition. She couldn't know he was there. Still, Flint felt as if she was staring right at him. His hand hovered above his teleportation beam, and he hesitated for one moment. Should he go down there and ask her? Should he tell her what he was about to do?

He had read the message she sent to the IDA. He knew she wanted this. Needed this. And even through the ship's camera, he could see the desperation in her eyes. He couldn't do anything but help. He got a lock on her in the teleportation beam and activated it.

Your rescue is here, Liza.

Now to go meet his match.

2

Liza chucked the trash into the trash can and winced as the lid slammed shut.

Dad would throw a fit if he heard that all the way in the house. Luckily, it was after eight, which meant he was down at Dancing Dollies, the sad little strip club off the side of the highway. Did he have the cash to throw money at those girls? Not really.

A thousand extra bucks a month would probably help a lot with his favorite pursuit.

Liza was still steaming mad about it. But standing out in the crisp night air washed away some of that anger. It really was a beautiful place. The mountains rolled out all around her. And when she tipped her head up to look at the sky, she got a really good idea of just how small, how insignificant she was. The Milky Way stretched out forever, millions of stars and galaxies beyond that.

She would miss this sky. This view. If she ever got up the courage to leave home, that was.

Already she was wondering if it was really that bad to pay rent to her dad. A thousand bucks a month was expensive for a shared room in the Valley. But it wasn't like she'd have other expenses. Except for the expense of taking care of his sorry ass.

She heaved a sigh and gave one last look up at the stars that kept her company on so many sad nights.

What was that?

There was a small ... smudge ... in the sky right above Mr. Grady's house. Was it smoke? But no, she didn't see anything like that, and the burning smell didn't tickle her nose.

She blinked and shook her head and couldn't see the strange blur anymore. Probably just her eyes playing tricks on her.

Liza turned to go back to the house and staggered as bright light washed over her and froze her in place. It didn't feel like any time passed. She blinked one second and opened her eyes the next, but she wasn't in her yard anymore. She couldn't smell the faint whiff of trash from the trash cans. There was no overpowering and refreshing scent of night air and green trees.

Instead, it smelled kind of antiseptic. Like a hospital. Or laboratory. The walls around her were bright white and her heart plunged into her stomach before jumping right back up and beating madly. What the hell was this? Where was she?

She lunged forward, distantly grateful that she wasn't tied down to anything. There was a door only a step in front of her, and she pounded on it, as if this might just be some sort of mistake, as if she had been found unconscious on her driveway, rushed to the hospital, and they forgot they stuck her in this weird little closet.

The door wouldn't budge.

Had she been kidnapped? Was she being trafficked somewhere? Would anyone realize she was gone?

The thoughts came at her a mile a minute. She couldn't make sense of any of it, and she wasn't sure that this was all some terrible dream.

With the door not moving, she frantically searched for anything she might use as a weapon. If anyone tried to kidnap her, they wouldn't find her an easy victim.

Her hands trembled, and she curled them into fists to hide the weakness. But there was nothing in the room. It was an empty closet.

What the hell was going on?

There was a click at the door, and it slid to the side with a whoosh. Liza scrambled out and glared at the person standing in the middle of the room.

He was really freaking hot.

What the hell, Liza? her mind screamed at her. Now was not the time to be finding weird kidnapper dudes kind of sexy. But he was. Dark hair, cropped close. Large, playful eyes and grinning mouth. Muscles. Lots of muscles. She liked those. She imagined if he took his strange black clothing off, she might see a six pack or something approaching one.

He looked like the kind of guy who could scoop her up, hold her close, and keep her safe from the rest of the world.

Now she knew for a 100 percent fact that she had gone cuckoo bananas.

Whoever this guy was, he was up to no good. She took a step back, but before she could retreat farther, she hit the door that had quietly closed behind her.

No escape. Not that running into a tiny closet would give her much escape.

"What the hell's going on?" she demanded. Maybe there was some kind of explanation for this. Maybe she had ... She couldn't figure out anything approaching logical for what was going on right now.

The man said something, but the syllables made no sense. She wasn't the most worldly person, but she had Netflix. She'd watched a Korean drama or two. She could recognize several languages, even if she could only speak English.

Whatever he was speaking, it was nothing she'd ever heard before. There was a lilt to it, and a bit of a trill. Almost as if he was a bit Scottish. But then there was a click in the back of his throat, and she didn't think Scottish people had clicks in their language.

Wasn't their language English?

Now was not the time to be pondering that.

"Who are you?" she demanded again as if that might magically make him understand her.

In her desperation, she looked around the room they were in. It looked futuristic, like something out of a sci-fi show. Almost like a spaceship, or what she imagined a spaceship to be, rather than what they actually look like from what she had seen on documentaries. It was all sleek, and white, and covered in buttons and switches. Was she in Star Trek?

Strangely, it reminded her a little bit of a sports car, though that might have just been the chair in the middle of the room. It belonged in a Maserati.

The hot guy took a step towards her, and Liza dodged to the side, giving up on backing into the room she had magically appeared in.

No, not magic. Magic didn't exist. She had probably been drugged or something.

But that didn't make it better. She searched for a weapon in here, but there was nothing. Nothing but her fists and her wits.

Well, at least she still had those.

But somehow the man managed to box her in, and he stepped closer, so close she could spit in his face.

But she was frozen right there, unable to move. Unable to react.

And she didn't think he was doing anything to keep her still. It was her own body that was rooted in place, strangely captivated by the man who was smiling at her like she was some sort of wild animal he was trying to save.

No one had ever accused her of being a feral cat

before. He raised his hand, and she flinched, and something like pain crossed his expression.

Oh, did it hurt the big bad kidnapper when she was scared of him? Too freaking bad.

He pressed something behind her ear and pain—no, *sound*—exploded in her head.

"There, there," the stranger said. "You're going to be okay." He placed his hand on her wrist.

She didn't know how she could understand him now. She didn't know what weird shit he was doing to her. And she wasn't going to waste time trying to find out. Liza reared back and punched him in the face with all of her might, yelping in pain as she bruised her knuckles against the hard bones of his cheek.

But it made him step back.

There was a giant red button in the middle of the display in front of his chair, and she ran for that. Giant red button. Emergency. Made sense to her. Maybe that would get her out of this mess.

Or at the very least it would mess up his day, and that was better than nothing.

She went for it, slamming her hand down and then pressing twice more when the man yelled in shock and outrage.

The room around them rocked, and suddenly Liza's ears popped, and the floor fell out from under her. She clung to the chair, knuckles white from the force of her grip, and realized she might have just made things a hell of a lot worse.

3

Flint let out a curse as the ungrateful woman he was supposed to be rescuing slammed down a second time on the teleportation button and the ship rocked dangerously, a sure sign they were in unsafe territory. The proximity alarm began to blare, and he had no more time to swear.

He had to act.

Liza gripped the back of the pilot's chair as the ship jolted around them, rocking wildly as if it had been locked into orbit and was being sucked in.

He had a sinking feeling that was exactly what was happening.

Were they heading back to that volcano planet? He might have been a dragon, but lava could still burn him to a crisp. And the human with him would be even more vulnerable.

He pressed a few of the buttons, trying to get a report about where they might be going, but he must have pressed the wrong thing. He really needed to get a better understanding of these controls.

One thing he knew how to do was manually pilot in a crisis. He grabbed the controller and took over, flicking the viewport to see what was in front of him.

Something crashed behind him as Liza lost her grip on the chair. The gravity field wasn't working. Or the planet had strong enough gravity that they were already feeling it. Concern jolted through him, but he couldn't worry about her right now. Not when they were in the middle of plummeting down onto some unknown planet.

Would they even be able to breathe?

Some rescuer he was.

Behind him, Liza grunted in pain, and his heart hurt for her, but he couldn't spare a second to look back and see how she was doing. Not if he wanted them both to survive the landing.

With her not strapped in, it was more dangerous than ever. But if her reaction to arriving on his ship told him anything, it was that she had a strong survival instinct. Even if she seemed to think he was abducting her rather than rescuing her. If she knew it was good for her, she would hold on.

The ship rocked even more as they hit the atmosphere, his heat shields screaming a warning that they were close to being compromised.

He didn't have another choice. They were in it now. And any atmosphere, at least, meant that they might have a chance of surviving. If they had air. If they had water.

They made it through the atmosphere, and his limbs felt heavier as real gravity took over for the artificial kind. His ears popped again, and he could feel the ship hurtling in free fall, rather than the gentle glide they needed to set down somewhere safe.

He grit his teeth and pulled on the controls with all his might, as if his own personal strength was what it took to get them to land safely. But he had dealt with dangerous landings before. He could deal with this.

The only mystery was where exactly they were. His coordinates were going haywire, probably something in the wiring broken. The life support scan, though, told him they had air and water. That was one bright spot in otherwise terrible news.

And the viewport told him they were in the

middle of an ocean. Not great. He had floatation devices he could deploy to keep the ship from sinking, but that would make the repairs all the more difficult.

He scanned his readouts for any sign of land and let out a yelp of joy when he spotted a small island. Small didn't do it justice. Tiny. Barely twice the size of the ship, and battered by roiling waves on all sides.

It was little more than a rock in the middle of the sea. But that was all he needed. If they could figure out how to get his ship space worthy again it wouldn't matter where they landed. As long as they *could* land.

It was a bumpy landing. Flint jolted in his seat, and he heard Liza smack into something. He gave the final safety checks the most cursory look, concern for her finally overwhelming everything else.

He was out of his chair in a flash and crossed the room to kneel over her.

Her eyes were closed, hiding the gorgeous brown orbs he'd been staring at since the moment he saw her. Her brown hair was tangled around her face, and there was a small bruise starting to form on her temple. If the med bay had survived, he could get her some healing gel and fix her up in no time.

With her eyes closed, she looked gentle. Not like the kind of woman who would come out of the teleportation chamber screaming. Screaming and raring for a fight. It was kind of hot. In a confusing sort of way. Flint always liked strong women who gave him a challenge. But that didn't mean he wanted to abduct them.

He was really going to have to figure this out.

Liza's eyes fluttered open, and she looked up at him with a soft smile that made something in his heart clench.

Then she most likely remembered where she was, and the expression slid off her face, replaced with a glare. She pushed him away and scrambled back, but he didn't miss the wince as she stood up.

He needed to get her medical attention. Just to make sure nothing was wrong.

"Whatever you want, I'm not giving it to you," Liza spat as she scrambled to her feet. She held her hands up in front of her as if she might punch him again.

The rush of adrenaline from landing the ship had overpowered the sting of his skin. Now his jaw was starting to throb, and he was mildly impressed with how much power she put into it. He would need to tend to her knuckles as well.

He didn't understand why he was so concerned for her. Sure, he was her rescuer. He had taken this job in the hopes something might blossom between them. They could go on an adventure together. One that was planned, not this surprise mystery destination. But he wanted to care for Liza so much that it was overpowering all the rest of his senses.

That didn't make sense. Not unless she was his

...

Now he was getting ahead of himself.

"My name is Flint," he told her. Maybe an introduction would make things better. "I got your message."

She scrunched up her face and glared even harder. "My message? What the hell are you talking about? Where are we? Are you a sex trafficker?"

He jolted as if shocked. "What?"

"I'm not doing freaky sex stuff," Liza insisted.

"I never asked you to." Now Flint was the one on unsteady feet. What world had she come from that she thought her rescuer might ... That was horrifying. He was no slaver. He only wanted to help.

Without warning, Liza lunged down the hall on the opposite side of the room. Flint chased after her, but she was fast. Whatever hurt she had endured, clearly it wasn't stopping her. But there was no exit this way. Not unless she went all the way to the other end of the ship and opened up the cargo hold.

At least, there wasn't *supposed* to be a door this way.

The giant tear in the hull on the side of the ship that exposed them to the salty sea air worked just as well. Liza shimmied through it.

With a curse, Flint followed after her.

"Just leave me alone!" Liza screamed at him. Her words were swallowed up by the wind and the waves around them.

And now Flint was getting a bit angry. She wasn't even going to let him explain the situation? "You sent out a rescue beacon!" He could feel his own fire bubbling in his veins, the smoke that wafted off an angry dragon singeing his nose.

Liza glared, and if she saw the smoke, she must not have realized what it was. "I didn't do any such thing. I don't need rescuing. I am a grown woman." She crouched down and picked up a loose rock from the surface of the island.

Flint froze where he stood. He didn't want to get pelted by the rock. No use making the situation any worse.

"I can explain ... I think." They just needed to have a conversation. Once they did that, this would all work out. They would figure out how to get off this weird little planet and clear up the situation.

Had he rescued the wrong woman?

He was definitely going to have to fill out a lot of paperwork from the IDA if that was the case.

But before Liza could respond, or he could figure out how to start, a massive creature, something that looked like a shark crossed with a lizard jumped out of the water and swept up Liza in its claws.

Liza screamed as she was pulled under the water.

4

LIZA DIDN'T HAVE time to suck in a deep breath before the strange monster dragged her under the water. She thrashed against him, fighting desperately against his claws, lungs burning, and eyes shut tight.

Was this really the end? Would she really die being dragged under water by some sort of mysterious beast?

She wasn't giving up that easily.

Her head felt like it might split open as fear and desperation rushed through her veins. Her terror was so powerful that she could feel her skin tingling where the monster pressed against her. She tried to scratch, but the thing's skin was weird. Scaly in some places, smooth in others.

In the one second where she got a look at him

before breathing became her only focus, she had the strangest impression of a dragon mixed with a shark.

She was going crazy.

At the exact moment she was sure her lungs would give out, when she couldn't keep her mouth closed anymore and had to suck in a breath, even if that breath would mean her end, they burst through some weird wall in the water and the water washed away, replaced by air.

An air bubble?

If Liza was going to survive this, she had to push the questions aside until she was safe. Or safer than she was right now with a monster intent on eating her.

The shark-dragon-man let go of her for a moment, and Liza had the opportunity to take him in. Her eyes widened in terror. It was humanoid in form yet undeniably malevolent, with almost luminous blue skin stretched tightly over a powerful frame and two arms ending in clawed hands.

His head was completely bald, and when he opened his mouth to growl, all she could see were rows upon rows of razor-sharp teeth glinting in the subdued light. His snout seemed to be shrinking as if the air around him had a transformative effect on his flesh, changing it from strange beast to more humanlike monster.

He stalked closer, looming over her menacingly with a growl vibrating from his throat like thunder. She felt small next to him, peering up at a figure that seemed to go on forever. Taller than any human she'd seen except for maybe the tallest basketball player ever. Seven feet? Eight?

Liza wasn't about to get out a ruler to check.

The monstrosity of a man lurched forward. "Mate!" He swiped forward, giant claws on his hands aiming for her clothes.

Mate? Not a chance in hell.

Letting instinct drive her, Liza did the only thing she could think to do when confronted with a shark. She slammed her fist into the dragon shark's snout.

It was the same hand that she had used to punch her kidnapper earlier, and she let out a yelp of pain as the impact reverberated up her arm.

The dragon shark froze as if stunned. There was no way it would last for long. Mind racing with fear and more than a little confusion, Liza looked for an escape. It looked like they were floating in an air bubble, but that couldn't be right. There were rocks on the ground, and driftwood. Had those things also floated in through the bubble? Could it collapse around her at any moment?

She sucked in deep breaths of air as if she could store it for later.

She didn't see a way out.

Her water dragon man made another sound at her, whatever had stunned him was wearing off right then.

There was driftwood at her feet, and Liza scooped it up, holding the branch like a baseball bat. If that thing got within two feet of her, she was swinging. If she couldn't stop it from ... She didn't want to consider what he might do to her when he called her mate.

But if she couldn't stop him, at least she would make him hurt.

A hysterical laugh escaped her throat, and for just a minute Liza wished she was back home, back in her father's house where he yelled at her for leaving dishes in the sink and demanded insane rent payments. She knew how to handle that. She could deal with his tempers and his demands. She'd been doing it her entire life. And never once had she been threatened with being eaten by a weird shark dragon monster thing. There was nothing familiar about this world or this creature.

She was going to die here. No help was coming. How *could* anybody help her? She didn't know where she was.

This was not any place on earth. Had she been abducted by an alien?

Thinking while she was supposed to be fighting for her life was going to get her killed even faster.

Maybe she could jump out of the bubble. She could swim desperately for the surface and hope she made it in time. But she wasn't quite sure which way was up and the dragon had swum underwater with way more speed than she could ever hope to match. If she left the bubble, she would drown.

"Mate!" the shark dragon screamed and charged.

But before he could come get closer, her own original kidnapper burst through the air bubble and shot fire out of his hands and mouth. The flames roared toward the shark dragon, filling the cave with a blast of heat so intense that Liza had to dive away as the fire swept over them.

5

Flint knew how to fight a dragon, but he'd never tried it underwater before. Instinct had seen him dive into the roiling sea after Liza, and some force he couldn't describe showed him his path, down and down and down into the depths.

The IDA hadn't undersold the adventure part of this mission.

He burst through an air bubble, fire blazing, and aimed straight for the creature who'd stolen Liza away from him. It was his duty to protect this woman, and he wouldn't rescue her only for her to be abducted by some alien monster.

Fire blasted from his mouth, from his hands. He took satisfaction in the roar of pain that erupted from the creature, but it didn't last for long. The shark dragon recovered quickly, and Flint barely managed to duck to the side before a spray of water shot out from its mouth. The stream looked powerful enough to cut a man in half.

He couldn't afford to glance at Liza as the deluge threatened to destroy him. All his focus went into dodging and attacking and moving. The water dragon was strong, but it wasn't fast, and that was his advantage.

Flint shot another jet of flame at the monster's face. It roared with rage, but before anything could make contact, the creature made a shield of water in front of himself to deflect the attack.

Smart beast.

Flint cursed.

He had to end this quickly if he wanted to save Liza's life. He had no idea how long the air bubble would hold, or if they could make it to the surface before either of them drowned. He wouldn't risk it.

He roared with the ferocity of his dragon form but didn't dare shift. The bubble was small, and he'd crush anything in his path. Including Liza. He couldn't risk it.

The shark dragon bellowed again, but this time its voice sounded different, deeper, more threatening. It opened its maw wide, as if it was about to bite. Flint stared down at an unending row of needle-sharp teeth.

Great.

His teeth could cause a grown man to tremble—in his dragon form. Right now, he was wishing he could summon them, but wishing in the middle of a battle was a good way to get dead.

The water dragon surged towards him, and Flint threw himself backwards, flinging fire as he went. His fire went straight through the bubble, but no water gushed in.

They might just survive this after all.

The water dragon was right over him now, and Flint gathered up all the power within him and shot all the fire and fury he could muster right at the water dragon's chest.

For a second, it was blinding. His vision whited out with the intensity of his own power. The force of the fire sent the water dragon shooting back and back and back until he hurtled out of the air bubble around them.

Ha!

A shot of triumph sang in his veins. But it didn't last.

Flint heard the trickle of water first, and that trickle quickly turned into a roar as the bubble started to dissolve where the water dragon had fallen through.

With a curse, he raced across the floor and found Liza gripping a piece of driftwood like a weapon and glaring with enough rage in her eyes to burn just as powerfully as his fire.

Good woman.

There was no time to explain. He grabbed onto her arm and followed the path where the water was rushing, hoping that, like a river, they were headed downstream to somewhere safe.

"Hold your breath!" he told Liza, who sputtered at the command.

Flint would apologize later. He dove under the water, still holding her arm, and swam down a tunnel for nearly a minute before he crashed through another air bubble, this one bordering the edge of an underwater cave.

Perfect, almost like he'd planned it.

He pulled Liza up and hugged her close, but she tore out of his grip, spitting mad, and would have definitely hit him with the driftwood bat if she hadn't lost it along the way.

She glared, but couldn't speak, instead heaving in deep breaths of humid, cold air. She was shivering, and Flint wanted to gather her close to warm her up.

He had a feeling she might disembowel him if he tried.

He liked her.

"What the hell is going on?" she asked, voice scratchy from screaming. "What is this place? What was that? Who are you? What do you want with me?"

The questions crashed over him as strong as the wave from before. "My name is Flint; I came to rescue you." He'd said it before, but that might have gotten lost in the whole being swallowed by a water dragon thing.

"Rescue me from *what*?" She wrung some of the water out of her shirt and clutched her arms around herself to stop the shivering.

Flint didn't see anything he could use to keep a fire going, but he summoned flame to his hand anyway and hoped the warmth might spread.

"How the hell—" Liza reared back, stepping away from the flame and defeating the whole purpose of him summoning it.

He kept it up anyway and hoped she might lose a bit of her fear. "You contacted the IDA," he reminded her. "You said you wanted to escape."

Her mouth dropped open and her eyes widened. "You're IDA? That's impossible. IDA's a support group ... or something. I was never quite clear on that." The last bit seemed to be said for herself.

"The Intergalactic Dating Agency—"

"Dating?!" That had her scurrying even farther back. At this point, she'd never warm up.

Clearly Flint was doing this all wrong. Asher and Knox made the whole thing look easy. What was he screwing up?

"Let's take a step back," Flint suggested. "I think there's been some sort of misunderstanding ..."

"A giant water monster just tried to ... mate ... me, you are holding fire in your hands like it's nothing, and some—did you say Inter*galactic*? Am I ... Are you ... aliens!" It wasn't quite a question, but he understood the gist.

"I'm from a planet called Vemion. I'm a dragon. And, yes, that means that, to your way of thinking, I'm an alien. The universe is a lot bigger than you ever imagined." He was handling this all wrong, he was sure. But how else was he supposed to handle it? "We need to find a way to the surface, to get back in my ship and go ... somewhere else."

Something told him she wasn't quite ready to meet his parents.

Liza looked at him like he'd grown a second head. "No way in hell."

"What?" She couldn't be serious.

She backed up another step and then looked over her shoulder and smiled faintly. "Look, thanks for saving me from that weird water dragon shark thing. I'm glad I wasn't eaten. But you kidnapped me, or did you forget that? I'm not going anywhere with you. And did you forget about the giant gaping hole in the side of your ship—your *space* ship, oh Jesus." She shook her head, as if trying to clear away the thought. "Nope. Not doing that."

She wouldn't listen if he explained the self-repair capabilities of his craft. Even the most enthusiastic spacer's eyes glazed over when he went into the healing properties of the metal and nanobots.

"Also, there's like a 63 percent chance that I'm in the middle of a nervous breakdown after my dad ... after whatever. So, I don't need or want your help anymore, okay? You head back to your ship or do whatever the hell you want. I'm going to go down this passage and see what I can find. Have a nice life. Or don't. I can't say I care."

Now that she mentioned it, he could see the split in the cave. A narrow passage lead right, a slightly wider one lead left. Or he could head back through the air bubble and try to swim for the surface.

Liza flicked her fingers in a dismissive wave. "Have a nice life, dude. Just don't follow me."

Flint let her go. He watched her retreat down the wider path and wished he could send his fire after her to keep her warm.

He knew nothing about this planet except for the monsters that lurked on it. Liza couldn't hope to survive. Still, he forced himself to wait several minutes before he followed after her.

6

It was stupid to go alone. Liza realized that almost immediately, but she refused to turn around and beg for Flint to stay by her side. She wasn't going to admit that she was in over her head.

Of course, just about anyone would be in over their head in the situation. Abducted by some fire-shooting douche. Then further kidnapped by a water dragon. And now stuck in the caves under some kind of alien ocean. She couldn't wrap her mind around it.

Although, she wouldn't say no to some fire breathing powers of her own at this moment. She shivered against the chill in the air, her wet clothes clinging to every curve and making matters worse.

Was she going to die down here?

The question was starting to get old. If every

time she ran up against a challenge and convinced herself she was going to die, eventually she would.

She had to find a way back to the surface. Or to find some *nice* water dragon guys who might lend her a hand. The kind of guys who wouldn't kidnap her or try to claim her has their mate or whatever. No, thank you. She didn't want any of that.

Even though there was a tiny, *miniscule* part of her that *maybe* appreciated how Flint looked. Liza groaned in frustration and clenched her jaw. She wasn't going to think about how hot he was, hot in a way that had nothing to do with fire. He'd kidnapped her. He didn't get hot guy privileges.

The cave tunnel seemed to go on forever. Liza's legs ached, and her whole body felt heavy, but that might have had something to do with the cold.

When did hypothermia start to set in?

She pushed the thought out of her mind. She had no way to warm up. No way to make a fire—and she refused to think about Flint and his magic hands at that moment—and she had to keep moving to find some way to survive. Liza had gotten through a lot of life being stubborn and willing to suffer; this was no different.

But after a while, she had to take a break. She found a decent sized rock and collapsed down onto it, sucking in deep breaths, and hoping she could find the strength to stand back up and keep going.

What would happen when she got hungry? She hadn't seen any sort of animal since she started down this path.

But there was evidence of something. There were regular scratches on the wall that looked too deliberate to be natural. She even caught a few that looked like cave paintings.

She hoped someone lived in these caves. Someone nice. Someone who could help her.

There was a large piece of driftwood about the size of a walking stick beside the rock, and Liza picked it up. She used it to heave herself up and start walking again.

She wasn't going to find anyone by sitting still.

She'd only gone a few feet when she heard a scuffle up ahead followed by a woman's yelp. Liza found the energy she'd been quickly losing and sprinted forward only to find a human woman caught between two of those dragon men. But these dragon men looked more human than the one who had taken her. Their snouts weren't as protruding, though their teeth were just as sharp. Their hands were mostly human, though their nails gave the suggestion of claws.

But it was two on one. And both those guys looked to be about seven feet tall.

Liza didn't hesitate. She bashed the closest one over the head with her walking stick, and he went down.

The woman must have hit the other guy in just the right place because he fell to the floor with a grunt as well.

The woman flashed Liza a grin. "Thanks for the help. Let's get out of here." She nodded further down the tunnel and started moving.

With not much other choice—she wasn't about to wait for the guys to wake up—Liza followed. The woman introduced herself as Samantha, and her long strides meant Liza had to take a few jogging steps to keep up.

"Where are we?" Liza asked. Her teeth chattered as she spoke, her jaw aching. "I crash landed here. Some giant water shark guy tried to—"

"You survived the wild dragons?" Samantha interrupted, eyes wide.

"Is that what they're called?" He had definitely been wild. Feral, perhaps. Nothing Liza wanted to see again. "I'd be happy to never see one of those guys again."

Samantha nodded in sympathy. "My house isn't

too far from here," she said. "And those two," she threw a glare back over her shoulder as if the men who had accosted her could feel it, "shouldn't have been here. This isn't their territory. Nereus won't like that."

Whether it was the cold, sleep deprivation, or the complete weirdness of this situation, Liza was having trouble processing everything Samantha said. "Nereus?"

Samantha smiled softly. "This is his territory. He rules this section of the underwater caves. And he's territorial about it."

"Are you human?" It felt kind of rude to ask it that way. Liza never thought she would have to ask that question before. People were human. That was just how it worked on earth. But clearly, everything was different now.

That made Samantha laugh. "I am," she confirmed. "I fell through a portal. Still not sure how it happened. I'm from Miami."

"Then I guess you're used to the beach." It was a nonsensical thing to say, but it sent both of them into roiling laughter.

Samantha's house, as she called it, wasn't so much a house as it was a built-up cave. There were crude walls dividing spaces, and there was a sort of yard to the side of it where washing hung to dry, and overhead there were narrow but long tubes in the ceiling of the cave that showed the water overhead and allowed light to trickle in.

"How does this work? Why aren't these caves flooded?" Liza was glad for the air, but this whole place didn't make sense, nothing did anymore.

"Nereus tried to explain it to me once," Samantha said. "It was kind of complicated and involved a lot of physics. Basically, there are some natural geysers in the caves, and the air pressure and water pressure meet. I don't know. It just works." She shrugged.

Without any other option, Liza accepted the explanation.

Samantha opened the thin wooden door to the house. "Let's get you some new clothes. You need something dry."

Inside the house, Sam shoved a bundle of fabric Liza's way. It was a flowy dress that belonged on the cover of an old-fashioned romance novel, the kind with barbarians and ripped bodices.

Liza stepped into a small bathroom and peeled off her old clothes and was grateful for the dry fabric. But when she picked up her old pants, she froze.

There was a strange gash on the calf. It looked almost like fire had singed it. But her leg was completely untouched. How could fire burn her clothes and not her skin?

Maybe if she had stuck with Flint, she would have an answer to that.

But frankly, Liza was more comfortable with Samantha.

She hung the clothes outside to dry while Samantha prepared a snack of strange fruits that Liza didn't recognize. She had a moment to wonder if she should eat. Was she like Persephone in the old story? Pulled down into the underworld and bound there by six pomegranate seeds?

Liza's tummy rumbled, and she decided eating would be just fine. No one had ever accused her of being a goddess.

Samantha had questions about Earth. Some of them Liza could answer. But the more specific ones about Miami were out of her purview. Liza was just figuring out what she needed to ask Sam about this planet, or whatever it was, when the front door to the dwelling slammed open, and a seven-foot-tall water dragon stalked inside.

He was more human, just like the ones who attacked Samantha earlier. He took a deep breath inside and a roar bellowed out of him, loud enough to hurt Liza's ears.

There was some sort of blue jewel, perhaps a sapphire, embedded in his chest right under the hollow of his throat. But Liza didn't have time to wonder about that.

The dragon man marched forward and backed Samantha up against the wall, both hands trapping her on either side.

"Who dared to touch you?" he bellowed.

Liza might as well not have been there.

Her hands ached for her driftwood staff. She could show this guy exactly how she dealt with overbearing assholes. But Sam's eyes got a bit glassy, her breath coming fast, and her nipples visible under the thin fabric of her top.

She was into this dude.

Something soured in Liza's stomach. What was it some women liked about assholes?

If Samantha answered the man's question, Liza didn't hear it. Between one second and the next the two threw themselves at each other, Samantha wrapping her legs around the man's thick waist as he hefted her into his arms and slammed their mouths together.

Samantha let out a breathy moan, and Liza looked away.

But she could still hear them. And she was only human. Of course her body started to react.

Liza slipped outside. No way was she getting caught in some weird under the sea threesome.

7

FLINT HAD STAMINA, but Liza's determination to keep on the move was a challenge even for him. When he passed a bend in the cave where the dirt was disturbed and a scuffle had clearly taken place, he found a new reservoir of strength to keep moving. If anyone had dared to hurt her, he'd rain down the fires of Vemion and make them pay.

His instincts were leading him on, pulling him forward down the tunnel of the cave, though he couldn't say why. Something inside of Liza called to him, though that should have been impossible. Unless she was his mate, but Flint couldn't hope for that. And he probably shouldn't, especially not after he'd screwed up their meeting so much.

He took another turn and saw fabric hanging on lines strung up beside a cave with a driftwood door and several carved windows. Laundry. There was something so banal about it that he wondered for a moment if he'd lost his mind. Perhaps there was some hallucinogenic gas in the caves, and he'd been breathing it in for hours.

Or, more likely, he'd just found someone's house.

And what about Liza?

As he got closer, he recognized the dark blue fabric of the trousers and the thin black of her shirt hanging limply in the still air. The fabric was nearly dry by now, so she could have been here for a long time.

Or someone had taken the clothing from her. And she might be ...

No. Flint refused to believe it. She'd fought off the water dragon. She'd fought off *him*. She could survive a hike through the cave on her own.

Then he noticed the tear in the fabric of the trousers. Not a tear. A burn. A burn from his fire. It singed completely through, and there was no way she should have been able to walk on a leg burned by dragon fire.

He heard something slam inside the house followed by a feminine shriek.

Flint rushed forward and past another line of

drying clothes, only to see Liza right there, sitting on a boulder in a flowing, pale green dress, cheeks flushed and hands clutching her knees.

"Are you hurt?" It came out harsh, but he couldn't temper his words, the memory of the fabric still burned into his mind.

Liza furled her brow, but at least she didn't look angry at him anymore. "What?"

He knelt down in front of her and looked up. "I saw your trousers. Did I burn you? Are you injured? Do you need help?" The desperate need to keep her safe, keep her whole, clawed at him in a way he couldn't understand, but Flint was powerless to fight it.

"I'm fine," she insisted, but she made no move to push him away.

"You look flushed." Concern had him rooted in place. "Let me check your leg." His hand grazed the fabric of her skirt. "Please."

She gave a faint nod.

Flint was careful not to hike the fabric any more than he needed. This tentative truce felt like it could fall apart at any moment, while everything in his soul demanded that he tend to Liza. The skin on her calf was pale and unblemished, the only hint of damage was a bit of swelling around her ankles from the walking and a bruise that could have come from anywhere.

He checked her other leg, just to confirm it, too, was unharmed.

It wasn't possible. His fire could burn through solid stone if he applied himself. Human flesh? She should have been burned to a crisp. The only person in the universe his fire wouldn't harm—aside from himself—was his mate.

Could Liza really be his mate? Had the IDA found her so easily?

If she was, he had to find a way to undo the mess he'd made. But first, they had to get off of this planet and away from its watery dangers.

He had to pull back. There was no way in all the galaxies that she wanted his touch after the day they'd had. But he was so close to her, and, for the first time, she wasn't spitting vitriol.

Oh, if his brothers could see him now ...

But they had no place here. This was between him and Liza.

He let go of her dress, but before he could pull away, Liza's hand flashed forward and held his palm in place, right on top of her knee, the barest hint of fabric separating him from naked skin.

He jerked his gaze up, waiting for her to say

something, do something, but the flush on her cheeks only intensified, her grip on his wrist tightening.

A feminine moan carried out the window followed by the rhythmic sound that could only mean a hard fucking.

"They've been going at it for an hour." Liza's voice was breathy. "Am I a freak for listening?"

His own cock twitched at his could-be mate's voyeurism. He could see it more clearly now, the flush on her cheeks wasn't pain, it was arousal. Her whole body strung tight with need. "You're not a freak," he promised. "Everyone needs their pleasures."

The skin under her neck pulsed with her heartbeat, fast and hard.

He felt like there was some huge beast inside of him raring to explode out of him and claim this woman. It wasn't the dragon that lived within, this was something darker, something primal.

But Flint wouldn't succumb, not with Liza so vulnerable right now. He refused to take advantage.

He ran his hand over her fingers. They were cold. He held her hands between his own and hoped his own body heat was enough to warm her. If he knew for certain she was his mate, he would have warmed her with his flame, but he couldn't risk it. Not right now.

After a moment, he shifted his grip and raised her hand to his lips, gently kissing each of her fingers, her palm. He watched as her eyes grew darker, her pupils expanding to swallow the hazel of her iris.

She swallowed, then licked her lips, but she didn't pull away.

He pulled her other hand forward and pressed the same kisses to the pads of her fingers and the flat of her palms.

All the while, the noises from the couple inside the house grew more insistent.

Liza trembled, and it took all of Flint's strength to let go, to pull back, when all he wanted was to surge forward and capture her lips with his own. But he didn't. They'd barely had a conversation that didn't end in blows. Liza needed time.

And he needed to calm down.

His voice was husky when he finally managed to speak. "My ship can repair itself."

"What?" She shook her head as if she was coming out of a daze.

"Before we split up you spoke of the tear in the hull. It may take a few days for the ship to be sky worthy, but it should already be fixing itself, sealing any potential holes or cracks. We'll—I'll—be able to fly again soon. I can take you home. Or anywhere else you want to go. I swear to all the dragons of old that I didn't mean to abduct you. You're welcome to anything in my hold as restitution. I just picked up a passel of gems for my brother, they're yours if you wish." He didn't want to separate from her, didn't want to send her back to whatever horrible life she'd been living back on Earth, but if taking her back meant he could start over again and fix things, he'd do it.

Liza blinked a few times. The sounds from insider were quieter now. "Just like that?"

"I can admit when I've made a mistake. And I can apologize." This might go down as the weirdest day of his life, but Flint would do what he could to make it right.

Before Liza could respond, the front door near them burst open, and a large man looked at them, gaze commanding. There was a strange blue gem embedded in the skin of his chest, and the only thing covering him was a short, dark sarong tied around his hips. He had the air of satisfaction that came from a man who'd left his mate well-pleased.

"Both of you, come in," the man commanded. "We have much to discuss."

Was this who'd Liza had been imagining for the last hour? Jealousy reared, but then Liza leaned closer to him as she stood, and Flint couldn't deny the flare of male triumph that roared through him.

If the large man could sense what was going on in Flint's mind, he didn't say.

With little other choice, Flint and Liza followed him into the house.

8

Liza's blood buzzed with the memory of Flint's lips. He'd kissed her hand so tenderly, and she had to battle something needy inside of her that wanted to pull him close and beg for more. How weak was she that the smallest kernel of kindness had her like this?

Inside the house, Samantha looked exactly like a woman who'd been making sex sounds for the last hour. But the table was set with plenty of food, two benches flanking the low surface. "I didn't get a chance to introduce you," she told Liza, eyes flicking to Flint for a moment. "This is Nereus, my mate."

Nereus, the man who controlled this territory and battled others for it.

He was one of the water dragons, she understood, but there seemed to be different kinds. Some of them were more human, or, at least, more like people rather than animals. But there was still something animalistic, almost predatory, in the way Nereus kept hold of Samantha. Not that she seemed to mind.

Samantha sat beside her mate on the bench and let out an indulgent laugh as he pulled her closer, practically dragging her into his lap.

Why was that kind of hot?

Liza didn't want Nereus. Didn't want Samantha. But something about the naked lust between them had her on the edge of squirming. But when she sat down on the bench beside Flint, she was careful to keep space between them. He'd already scrambled her brains once. Liza couldn't let it happen again.

But she didn't miss the way he spread his legs just enough that they brushed up against hers. She didn't move, she refused to cede ground.

She selected some items that looked appetizing, mostly fish and some of the strange fruit she'd eaten before, all the while remaining silent. Nereus and Sam shared a plate, and half the time Nereus fed his mate from his own hand, rather than letting her eat for herself.

Did Flint really mean it when he said he'd take her home? That his ship could repair itself? She didn't necessarily want to go back to her father's house, but there was Erica to think about. Her sister would need her when her relationship with Troy fell apart.

Samantha was explaining how she'd met Liza to Nereus, and Flint listened with open interest. "The beasts who tried to take me weren't wild dragons."

"They'll pay for touching what's mine." Nereus nuzzled at her neck.

And the flush was back. These two needed to get a damned room.

"How do we get back to the surface?" Flint asked, voice a bit strained. At least she wasn't alone in being affected by the show.

The large water dragon didn't let go of his woman while he spoke. "There's a path. The way you entered is not the only way in or out, and it would be the most difficult way for you to return with no way to breathe underwater. I can lead you to the edge of my territory. It's another day's journey past that, and you'll be in wild dragon territory."

"I can handle wild dragons," Flint said. He held his hand up and let fire bloom.

Despite seeing it before, Liza was still impressed. It was kind of sexy, a man that could control fire. Not that she wanted to think about Flint as sexy.

Nereus's own expression turned interested. "I could use a man with your abilities. You and your mate are welcome to join my cause. I will sponsor you into my clan."

"Mate?" Liza jerked herself to the other side of the bench, putting as much space between herself and Flint as possible.

Flint didn't move, he also didn't look at her, as if she might turn to stone from a glance.

Samantha might be happy getting fucked by a giant monster-man, but that wasn't Liza. Years under her father's roof had her holding her tongue. She was almost grateful for the discipline. Samantha had been nothing but nice to her, and she didn't want to repay that with rudeness.

"I think," Flint finally said, "that if there's any chance of us leaving the planet, we want to take it. I need to get Liza home."

He could still be lying. Her dad lied in front of other people all the time, telling them how he'd offered to pay for dance classes when she was little, and she was the one that turned him down, telling them he wanted her to go to the state university as if he wasn't the one who'd forbidden her from making an application.

But she believed Flint. Maybe it was crazy.

Maybe she was deluding herself. But she wanted to believe him. She wanted to believe in something.

It wasn't long before Liza started to yawn while Samantha told Flint the story of falling through a portal and ending up in the middle of a ring of wild dragons while buck naked and a bit high for the first time on weed. Liza wanted to hear more, but it had already been nearing bedtime when Flint ... picked her up ... from Earth. How long had she been awake?

"I believe our guests are tired, my love," Nereus said. Samantha had somehow ended up completely in his lap, and he had a proprietary hand on her stomach.

Samantha winced. "Sorry. I ramble."

"No, it's really interesting," Liza insisted, but she cut herself off with a yawn.

"I'll show you to your room," said Nereus.

Liza would be a poor guest if she asked for a second room. How many bedrooms could a cave have anyway? The place was spacious, but very open.

"Our quarters are on the other side of this wall," Nereus said once he'd led them to where they'd be sleeping. "There is a bathroom just there." He pointed at another closed door. "If you need anything, just ask." And then he left them alone in the room.

Where there was only one bed.

In fact, the room was basically only bed. Liza might have offered to sleep on the rocky floor, but the space beside the bed was barely wider than her body, and there wasn't much room at the foot. The bed itself though was like two king beds pushed together. Maybe more than that. An entire orgy could happen in that bed, and she could sit on the edge and be unbothered.

Well, not unbothered. But untouched.

Why was she thinking about orgies?

"I can sleep on the ..." Flint trailed off, coming to the same conclusion she had.

"This thing is the size of a football field. I think we can share." She wasn't sure how he'd transformed from kidnapper to bedmate (platonic!) in the last few hours, but the day was too weird to question it.

Hopefully she'd wake up and realize this was all a very strange dream. Maybe she'd been slipped hallucinogenic mushrooms. That would explain a thing or two.

Nereus hadn't offered them any pajamas, and she got the idea that he and his mate didn't wear much in the way of clothing when they were alone. It made the fucking easier.

The dress was comfortable enough. Flint had taken off his boots when they entered, but still wore his salt-crusted pants and shirt from their underwater adventure.

As if summoned by her thoughts, Samantha knocked on the door and stuck her head in before they acknowledged her. She held out a large piece of fabric. "I should have offered to clean your clothes earlier, since I washed your ma—Liza's. You can wear this and change back in the morning."

Flint took the fabric and managed to put it on and strip off his clothes without flashing her.

And, god above, did he look sexy with just the dark blue sarong slung over his hips. She had to force herself to look away as heat seared through her. She'd never felt this kind of compelling attraction before, this want to get close and devour another person.

Definitely hallucinogenic mushrooms.

Flint made sure the knot on his sarong was tied very tight, then he tied it again around one of his legs, probably to keep it from gaping in the night. Gentlemanly behavior.

A part of her was disappointed.

"My brothers will want to kill me when they hear about this," he said once they were settled into the bed.

"They won't be happy you're safe?" Liza didn't have anyone she could tell, not unless she wanted to end up in the loony bin.

"They'll be ecstatic. And then they'll remember that I put myself in this situation in the first place and want to beat the adventure right out of me."

"They'd beat you?" These brothers didn't sound so good after all.

He laughed. "No, of course not. Nothing more than a tongue lashing. And then they'll tell our mother." He shuddered. "She's going to make me promise not to leave Vemion for a month. That's my home planet," he added at Liza's blank look.

"Tell me about your family." She wanted to soak it up, this man who could smile so broadly while talking about censure, about the way loving and being loved radiated off of him.

He did. She learned about his triplet brothers, and then the other siblings on top of that. He let slip that he was cousin to a freaking king and that his proper name was Lord Flint of Vemion.

Lord. Like in one of those historical romances her Aunt Claire loved to read.

He regaled her with stories until they heard a masculine groan next door followed right by a breathy, feminine moan. They both went silent.

Liza tried to ignore it, but her body was strung tight, all her emotions right on the surface, and she couldn't. She couldn't ignore the way Flint's broad chest looked in the dim light from the cave windows, couldn't pretend that the way he smiled at her didn't make her want stupid things she couldn't have.

"They sure are ... active," Flint said as the moans gave way to a steady pounding.

Her cheeks felt flushed. "Maybe we can ignore it?"

"We can try." His own voice came out strained.

Nereus and Samantha didn't stop.

Liza let her hand creep over, reaching out further than she expected. The bed was that big. But her fingers brushed against Flint's naked thigh eventually. He sucked in a ragged breath.

"We're not going to sleep if we're ... It would just be blowing off steam." Suggesting it at all probably meant she was going crazy, but Liza's body was smoldering with lust for the man beside her. It didn't have to mean anything.

Flint reached forward and took her hand,

running his thumb over her palm in soothing circles. "I want to kiss you."

The admission made her tremble. "I like kissing." She pushed herself a bit closer, as far as her brazenness would allow. There was still nearly a foot of space between them.

Until Flint rolled to his side and then went farther, ending up on top of her, his hands on either side of her head, his legs straddling her thighs. Their gazes locked, his own eyes seemingly lit with an inner fire. He gave her plenty of time to change her mind, to protest. She didn't.

His lips met hers.

Liza's eyes fluttered shut.

He smelled like sea salt and smoke, an exotic combination she'd never known she could crave. She opened her mouth, and he took full advantage, slipping his tongue in, a groan escaping him as if tasting her was the most exquisite pleasure.

She arched upward, seeking. She wanted him closer, but he didn't press down on top of her, just deepened their kiss further. His lips, his tongue, everything about him intoxicated her. It wasn't possible to get enough.

One of his hands traced down the side of her arm and rested on her hip. It would be so easy to lift up into his touch. But she had to remind herself that this was just a kiss. A stress relief. Something to help her get a good night's sleep.

As if she'd ever fall asleep after this.

She raked her fingers through his hair, delighting in the small hitch in his breath as he broke away from her mouth only to kiss down the column of her throat. Her pulse throbbed under her skin, and she whimpered when he nipped at her collar bone, his stubble tickling her skin.

It was still just a kiss, she told herself, just lips on skin.

If her legs hadn't been trapped by his, she might have spread them, might have begged for more contact. But he had her pinned beneath him. It wasn't something she'd ever imagined herself wanting.

The sounds from the other room grew louder. And then softer. Quieted altogether.

She didn't want their kiss to end.

His lips met hers once more, and he brought his hands up to cradle her face, touch her like she was fragile, precious.

When he finally pulled away, they were both breathing hard.

She could ask for more, she knew. He might even

give it to her. And then her whole head would be scrambled in confusion about what she was supposed to want and who she was supposed to be.

Flint rolled back onto his back. "Sleep well," he said.

Liza doubted she'd ever sleep again.

9

IF IT WEREN'T for the imminent threats that came from getting off this damned planet or the fact that his mate might leave him for good once they were safe, Flint would be buzzing with excitement and possibility. He could still taste Liza against his lips, even after a night of fitful sleep.

The way she'd responded to his touch was beyond anything he could have hoped. But he couldn't expect her to get over all of her reservations after one kiss.

A dragon could dream, though.

The sarong wrapped around his waist felt like it hid nothing, and every time Liza glanced at him, she blushed. Thankfully his clothes were folded in a clean pile outside the door to their room. He put them on quickly, feeling more like himself once his boots were securely tied to his feet.

Liza kept the dress, though she slipped on the shoes she'd been wearing when he took her from her home. Neither of them wanted to walk barefoot through these caves.

It was a pleasant morning. Nereus and his mate had taken a break from their rutting, and Flint thought he could have called them friends in another life. But this planet didn't care about the same technology he was used to, and they didn't seem to have interstellar communication abilities.

Samantha kissed Nereus when he announced it was time for the three of them to be on their way.

Liza and Flint hadn't spoken more than three words to each other since waking.

Another man, a stronger man, might have called the kiss a mistake. If his could-be mate shut down so completely after a kiss that *she* invited, he should take the hint. But then he'd catch her looking at him with a soft, wistful expression and hope would flare as strong as dragon fire.

He could have her. Somehow. He just had to figure out the way.

Nereus carried a heavily designed staff with a blue jewel that matched the one embedded in his chest. "Do all ... non-wild dragons have jewels like that?" he asked.

"We're called Abyssians," Nereus corrected. "And, no, that's not what separates us from wild dragons. My stone is ... something else. And our walk is nowhere near long enough to relay that story." He held his hand up to the gem but pulled away before he touched it.

Intrigued but properly warned off, Flint let the question drop.

Nereus wasn't much of a talker. He pointed out dangers in the territory and instructed them which plants were safe to eat. Other than that, he kept quiet.

Flint and Liza followed his lead.

After several hours of walking, when Flint's legs were starting to ache from the effort, Nereus called a halt. They were at a strange arch covered in indecipherable writing in the tunnel. "Rest here for awhile," Nereus said. "This is the last truly safe place you'll have until you reach your ship."

"End of the line?" Liza asked.

Nereus furrowed his impressive brow but nodded after a moment as he worked out her meaning. "I must leave you here. Leaving my territory at the moment would be unwise. And I've already left my mate alone for far too long."

"Thank you for bringing us here," Flint said.

"The path beyond is straightforward," their guide explained. "It will take you to the shallows. You'll know you're close when the cave starts to flood. Have no fear, it rarely gets more than a foot or so high. Wade through that, and you'll come out on the island where your ship must be."

"How do we know it's the right island?" Liza asked. She'd slumped down on a boulder and didn't look eager to get up. She took a drink of water from a skein Samantha had provided and then offered it to him.

"There's only the one above these caves. It's all connected, part of an ancient mountain of fire. Our land is large but submerged."

Flint nodded, trying not to think about just how close a call landing on this planet had been.

"If you meet a wild dragon, show no mercy. They cannot be reasoned with, and they will not spare you in their quest to get her."

Liza squeaked at that. "What?"

"They're beasts driven by the need to rut. They kill all males and capture females until they use them up. New wild dragons are born of those ... interludes. The females don't last long."

"Kill with extreme prejudice, got it." She shot Flint a look. "Got that, dragon man?"

Despite the horror of the possibility, he laughed. "You have my word, my lady."

Her cheeks flushed, and she had to look away. If Nereus noticed something, he didn't say.

"Good luck," Nereus said. The you'll need it went unspoken. He left them there after taking a few minutes to rest his own legs.

Once he was out of sight, Liza groaned. "Why can't there be a nice, simple, safe ... elevator or something to take us to the surface. My thighs are killing me."

Flint had to bite back an offer to massage them for her. "We're in no rush. Rest for as long as you need."

She harrumphed. "The longer we wait, the worse it's going to be. I guess I'm ready."

His own muscles protested, but he'd survived worse at the Vemion Military Academy. He expected to feel something—magic, static electricity, a change in temperature, anything—when they walked through the arch. But it was just an arch, probably an old demarcation between Abyssian territories.

He was on edge, senses straining to hear any threat that might come their way. No wild dragon would take Liza, not for any reason.

They walked for a long time. Liza grumbled a bit, but she didn't slow. Even Flint's considerable muscles were beginning to protest.

"I never thought I'd miss my dad's house," Liza muttered as they crossed a suspiciously muddy tangle of vines growing on the tunnel floor. It was too soon for them to be in the shallows. He wouldn't ask where the water for the mud came from.

"Is it not your home too?" He knew she'd begged the IDA for help—even if she hadn't realized it—but he didn't know what she'd told them beforehand. He wasn't entitled to that information just because he was her rescuer.

"It's the only place I've ever lived," she grumbled. "But my father is ... He sucks. He's always sucked. He was a bit better when my mom was alive, but even then, he sucked. Then she died, and he sucked even harder. My little sister ...," she trailed off.

"I know a thing or two about little sisters. Mine's named Remy, and the king had better watch out if he doesn't want to be efficiently usurped. She already did it to my brother." He regaled her with Remy's takeover of Asher's position on a colony of Vemion. She'd be governor one day, almost certainly, and he doubted her rise to power would stop there. His little sister was ambitious.

"You're a triplet and you have a younger sister?"

"Not just that. I have one older and one younger brother and an older sister. There's seven of us total. My parents wanted a huge family. They got it." His home had been something of a circus growing up, but he wouldn't trade a second of it, not even when Arlo had gotten the drop on him and locked him in a luggage trunk for an hour.

Liza grimaced. "I'm glad it was just the two of us. I'd never get out if I had more younger siblings. It feels like I've been waiting forever for Erica to get out, and now she's shacked up with a guy I'm sure is just like our dad. I can't—"

He wanted to pull her into his arms and offer what comfort he could, but Liza's shoulders were set tight, and she looked like a kind touch might shatter her. He kept his distance.

"Samantha reminded me of her, you know. They don't look anything alike, and personality-wise ... I don't know, maybe I was just looking for something familiar. Samantha seems happy enough with that overbearing dragon."

Flint doubted they'd seen every facet of Nereus's personality, but now was not the time to defend the man.

They kept speaking as they walked, conversation drifting from heavy topics to lighter ones. And as Liza opened up to him, Flint wondered if he really could have this woman as his own. If she really could be his mate. He wanted her so bad he burned with it. And every word she spoke wove a spell around him.

What could he do to make her say yes?

A wild dragon appeared from seemingly nowhere, roaring and rushing at Liza.

Flint cursed as he raised his hand and let out a blast of flame at the creature, hitting its shoulder and forcing it back. It roared again, enraged, and lunged at him, missing by mere inches.

The thing had to have been at least twice Flint's size. If it got a woman, it would tear her apart.

It wasn't getting Liza.

He sent more fire shooting its way. It leapt to the side, agile despite its size, but it still ended up singed. Good. He'd take care of the beast; there was no other choice.

He didn't see the other wild dragon coming. He only knew it was there when Liza screamed.

Flint felt a *yank* on his power, and suddenly heat filled the cavern as Liza took control of his power and lit the wild dragons up.

10

Liza didn't have time to think about how she was shooting fire out of her hands. The wild dragon went down, and then Flint was right there, and they took off running and didn't stop.

Shouldn't her hands be burnt?

Had Flint done it, and it just seemed like it was her?

The thoughts slipped away as fast as they came and before long, her feet splashed in ankle-deep water. The shallows. Just like Nereus had promised.

Her lungs burned, and she needed to rest, to suck in big gulps of air until her head was no longer buzzing with pain and adrenaline. But now the water was waist high, cold enough to make her teeth chatter, and leading towards a brightly lit opening.

They were right there.

What if they were surrounded by wild dragons?

They weren't. She and Flint scampered out of the cave and spotted the ship almost immediately. The tear in the side was gone, healed just like Flint said it would be. They raced to the door, and Flint opened it, waving frantically for her to get inside.

He went straight for the cockpit, and she followed after him. But when he took a look at the dashboard, he cursed. "The hull won't be stable for another few hours." He pressed one of the controls. "Add a few more hours to that. At least the defensive system is working. We don't want any wild dragons attacking us while we're here."

A few more hours until they went home.

Liza didn't want to go. Yes, she wanted to get back to Erica, wanted to make sure her sister was safe, make sure she had a place to land when everything with Troy went to hell. But if she was back, this whole nightmare would be over. This strange, unbelievable dream with a man who made her want things she'd never dared to crave.

She didn't know how to say any of that.

Flint pushed back from his seat and turned to face her. There was a smudge of dirt on his face, and his clothes were sopping wet. She shivered, realizing she was just as soaked.

"Are you alright?" Flint stalked forward, raising his hand to her cheek but pausing before he quite closed the distance.

Wasn't Liza allowed to want things for herself?

She took half a step, closing that gap and letting Flint's hand touch her. "I'm cold," she said. "And my clothes are wet."

His throat bobbed. "I can find some spare clothes for you."

Liza slid the straps of the dress down either side of her arm and let it fall to the floor in a heap of wet fabric. She stood there, naked before him except for her shoes, and felt totally exposed.

Fire flared in his eyes, and he groaned. Then he kissed her.

And she felt like she'd come home.

Flint cupped her face with both of his hands and tilted her head back to allow him access to plunder her mouth. He kissed like he wanted to consume her, to taste and explore every inch of her body. She felt alive with him, burning from the inside out with need for more.

It was dizzying. She had to hold onto his shoulders, letting his strength steady her. He wrapped an arm around her back, holding her tight against him. Liza let herself sink into him, revel in his warmth, in the proof that he wanted her.

He trailed kisses down her throat with little nips that made her gasp, made her toes curl in anticipation. He backed her against a wall and lifted her up, urging her to wrap her legs around his hips.

There was something deeply erotic about rubbing against his fully clothed form with her naked skin.

His lips on her bared breasts drove her mad. She arched against him, panting as he played with one nipple, rolling it with his fingers before sucking it into his mouth. His tongue teased her sensitive flesh, and then he grazed her with his teeth before switching sides.

She whimpered when he pulled away.

They'd almost died out there in the caves. One wrong move could have erased either of them, both of them, from the universe. And then she'd never know what it felt to be worshiped like this, taken by this man.

She didn't even care that he wasn't exactly a man, not in the way she'd understood that before yesterday.

She wanted the dragon to claim her.

He was content to play with her breasts, to tease her nipples until she was writhing in his grip. He kissed her mouth again, tongue sliding inside to stroke against her own.

Then she reached down, groping for his belt.

He batted her hand away, holding her firmly by the wrist as he growled against her. It was almost like one of the sounds Nereus had made, but so much hotter coming from Flint's throat. "Not yet." The words rumbled deep. And then she was suddenly being carried, clinging to this dragon like he was a lifeline.

He settled her onto the small couch in the back of the cockpit, one she'd barely noticed since the white material blended in against the white wall. He knelt between her legs and looked up, his eyes dancing with flames and desire.

"Yes?" he asked, lips brushing up the inside of her thigh, sending ripples of pleasure through her.

"God, yes." Her voice came out high, breathy. She sounded desperate and needy, and she didn't care.

Flint grabbed her legs, pushing them apart until he had room to breathe against her most sensitive place. She bit her lip, holding back a moan as he pressed his mouth against her.

And then he licked her.

She couldn't hold back her noises then, and he rewarded her with another lick, his tongue parting her folds and teasing her opening. She was already on edge, already trembling with the need for release, and he made her cry out again before he focused his attention on the swollen bundle of nerves that had her squirming.

The licking turned to sucking, and she rocked against his mouth as he tortured her, drawing out pleasure that made her writhe, made her beg for more. He kept going, stroking her with his fingers, with his mouth, making her cry out loud as her body trembled on the edge.

Then he stroked the flat of his tongue over her and she shattered. Her whole body spasmed, release pulsing through her as her inner walls clenched around nothing.

She needed more. Needed him to fill her.

Flint pulled back, and she reached for him, tugged him up close and laid back until he towered over her. "Please," she begged. "Please, I need you."

If he'd been planning to pull back, that was his destruction. With a groan, he captured her lips, and she could taste her own release. Somehow, he'd torn his shirt off, or maybe the heat emanating from him had burned it to ash. He shimmied out of his pants until he and Liza were mouth to mouth, skin to skin.

Her hands traced his muscles, marveling at his strength, his size. He was built like a god, and she'd never imagined she could have this kind of man, this kind of fantasy. He was fire and smoke and heat, and he burned only for her.

He brushed up against her sex, and she wanted to weep it felt so good. Her body was still strung out on her orgasm, but it didn't matter as need kindled deep. She cried out as he entered her, spreading her wide around him.

He didn't stop, just kept pressing in and in, filling her, stretching her. She whimpered when he finally bottomed out, her body shuddering around him, gripping him tight.

And then he pulled out and thrust back in.

She arched up into him, nails biting into his skin as he fucked her, taking her with a ruthless passion that she never realized she craved. He felt amazing inside her, and she tightened her muscles just to hear his breath hiss out.

She wanted this dragon with her entire body, wanted his claim on her skin, wanted to see him fall apart because of her.

She reached up and yanked his head down,

claiming his mouth for a kiss that left both of them gasping for air. He thrust in, harder, faster, and she felt herself climbing that precipice again.

His mouth fell to her throat, his breath hot against her skin. Her whole body shuddered, and she was so close, teetering on the edge. He reached between them, and his fingers found her sensitive bud, and it was over. She came, clenching around him, crying his name.

Flint stilled on top of her, moaning as her body gripped his hard cock tight. He throbbed within her, groaning out his own release.

He rolled them over until she was sprawled across his chest, and his arms came around her, keeping her close. Liza couldn't think, couldn't breathe, could only allow herself to be held, to bask in the intimacy.

She'd never felt anything like this before.

She snuggled in closer, running her fingers through Flint's hair, delighting in the sensation of his touch and the sound of his breath in her ear.

Her dragon.

That thought had reality rushing back in far too soon. She stiffened but refused to pull away. She'd earned this reprieve, even if it was only once.

Still, she couldn't forget their escape, the way

they'd narrowly gotten out of the caves. What she'd done.

"How did I shoot fire?" she had to ask.

And the answer, when it came, was almost expected, almost a relief. Even if she wasn't sure at all what it meant.

He tightened his arms around her. "It's because you're my mate."

11

Somewhere between making love to his mate and revealing who she was to him, Flint had made an error. There hadn't been much talking after that. The excitement of the fight with the wild dragon and all the energy they used getting back to the ship finally took its toll, and they both passed out.

It was a good sleep. Flint had never imagined what it would feel like to have his mate in his arms, but now he knew.

He didn't want to wake up alone. Yet, that was exactly what happened.

He could play things cool. He just didn't want to. She was his mate. He didn't want to play games or lie or do anything that put the potential of their bonding at risk.

Not any more risk than he'd already put it in.

But the ship was nearly ready to take off, and he had to put those worries aside for now. He and Liza would have time to talk once they were safely in space.

She wouldn't have anywhere to get away from him.

He probably shouldn't be thinking that way. He'd already kidnapped her once ... sort of. If she didn't want to talk ... No, he was going to talk to her. They had to hash this out. He wasn't leaving things unspoken. He had messed up enough already.

The water system was working, so he took the opportunity to wash off the worst of what the last two days had done to him. Fresh clothes made him feel like a new man, and he hoped that Liza had snooped around enough to find something for herself.

She was sitting in the cockpit when he returned. She gave him a polite look, not the kind of look he wanted from the woman who had blown his mind only a few hours ago, but she didn't run screaming, so perhaps that was good.

Were his standards too low?

"Did you sleep well?" he asked her. He took his seat in the captain's chair and read over the repair progress report.

"Do you think we'll be able to leave soon?" Liza asked.

Flint's jaw hardened. Were they all business now? Or maybe she was still trying to wrap her mind around everything that had happened in the past day or so. After all, she had only just learned about life on other planets. It had to be a lot to take in.

"A few more hours, I think. We're close." If wild dragons were bearing down on them right now, he probably could get the ship in the air. But there was no sense in risking it when the shields were holding and they seemed relatively safe.

Liza took a seat in the navigator's chair and studied the map in front of her. "Do you know how far we are from Earth?"

"Quite a distance." He still had to calculate that, since the jump had been basically random. It was pure luck they landed somewhere they could survive.

"What does quite a distance mean?" Her hand hovered over the star map.

"A few hundred light-years maybe?"

"That's not possible. Einstein says ... something. I'm not really sure how it's supposed to work. I think

I watched a show about space travel on PBS." She sighed. "Never went to college."

"I don't know who Einstein is," Flint admitted. PBS either, but that didn't seem as relevant. "And I couldn't explain the science behind the travel. My ship has the capability to jump between two points in space. That's how we cover the distance. Did you want to go to college?" He wasn't sure how education worked for people on Earth. He had the best tutors, then the military academy, and then he could have gone on to further study if he had been inclined. But Flint had just wanted to explore.

Liza studied the map in front of her some more. She didn't answer his question.

So, she got to ask questions and he didn't? It didn't seem fair. But Flint forced himself to tamp the frustration down. It had been an exciting two days. Everyone reacted differently to that.

Before he could ask anything else, the ship's communication system rang with an incoming message. He opened it and smiled when he saw his older sister, Nix, her youngest child, Saffron, and both of his parents on the video. "Tell Uncle Flint we miss him," Nix instructed her child.

"I miss you, Uncle!" Saffron waved at the video, fire sparking wildly at her fingertips.

She still had to learn control. Two years old was a dangerous age for a dragonling and all the combustible items in their home.

"We can't wait to see you," said his mom. "The royal banquet is coming up, and I expect you to be here. You're going to regale all of us with your tales of adventure, and I promise that I will only fuss over you for five minutes."

His father gave his mother a disbelieving glance and then winked at the screen.

They told him they loved him, and the video stopped.

Flint smiled.

Out of the corner of his eye he could see Liza looking at the screen. He glanced her way and caught just a glimpse of abject sadness in her eyes before her expression closed off completely.

From what she had said, her home life was nothing like his. But he could share this with her. His family could be her family. If only she would let him in.

He reached out a hand, compelled to wipe the sad look off her face. She ignored it.

"What did you mean when you said I'm your mate?" she asked. It wasn't in the kind of tone that said she was excited at the prospect.

Flint pulled his hand back and tried not to feel rejected, even though that's exactly what happened. "It means that you can't be burned by my fire. You can control it. If I were in my dragon form, we could speak mind to mind."

"Is that it?" Her arms were crossed, her whole body tight.

The question cracked at him like a whip. "Fate has marked us to be together," he said. "It's a rare gift." Some of his frustration bled into his voice.

"What? Am I the only one who can give you children or something? Can't get it up without me? Do you need me or ... I don't know ... food loses its taste or whatever?"

Each question cut like a knife. "It's an offer from fate, not a command." Flint would not be the one to force her into a bond if she didn't want it.

He tried to ignore the way it made his heart feel like it was breaking in two.

"Are you still going to let me go back home?" Liza asked, challenge in her expression.

So that's how it was. Flint leaned forward and set a course for Earth.

12

EARTH LOOKED BASICALLY EXACTLY the same when Liza climbed down the stairs from Flint's ship on the outskirts of town. The air was a bit crisper, fall fully setting in.

"It's been about two weeks." Flint joined her on the ground. "I know it didn't feel like that for us, but with our time on the other planet and the travel distance, that's how long you've been away." He held up a small pouch that sounded like it was full of pebbles clacking together and held it out to her.

The gems he'd promised as payment for accidentally kidnapping her.

If Liza was a slightly better person, she might have rejected the offering. She forced herself to grab the pouch and slipped it into her pocket. She didn't check what he'd given her. She trusted Flint enough that she knew he wasn't lying.

Was she really going to walk away?

Her heart was screaming at her to not do something so stupid. But her mind was fully in control right now. She didn't want to be forced to take care of someone else. And being his mate might turn out to be just that. She had spent her whole life doing it. Her father. Her mother when she got sick. Erica. She couldn't go from one caretaker role to another.

Besides, her sister needed her. Or she would. In two weeks, everything could have imploded between Erica and Troy.

Liza had to be there to pick up the pieces.

She looked at Flint and wondered if she should kiss him goodbye. But she feared if she started kissing him, she might never stop. That sex had been ... damn. The man knew what he was doing. And it lit her whole body up in pleasure.

If that was their first time, when neither of them really knew each other, when they didn't know what each other liked or wanted or needed, what would it be like once they had the opportunity to know each other's bodies? She wouldn't get to know. It was something she had to sacrifice to keep her sister safe. She had a responsibility. Flint could go back into the loving arms of his happy family and find someone new. It wasn't like he would die without her.

"Thanks for bringing me home," she said. Then she forced herself to turn away and started walking back to town.

It wasn't much of a walk. But a few minutes into it, Liza realized she didn't have anywhere to go. Her father's house was absolutely out of the question. He would throw a fit if she showed up two weeks after disappearing without saying a word. And then he would probably demand the cash for rent that he'd demanded before she left.

He wasn't getting a single freaking cent. She would have to figure out how to turn the gems that Flint had given her into cash. But that was a problem for another time.

Every step that she took away from Flint's ship felt fundamentally wrong, like some part of herself was being torn away and she was forcing herself to split her existence in two. Like she would be living less than half a life if she kept moving.

But Liza didn't stop. She couldn't just leave Earth, leave Erica. The only way she had ever left this town was literally being abducted by an alien.

Her alien mate.

She kept walking.

Erica and Troy rented a small apartment in an old house on the outskirts of town. The walls were thin, and Liza could hear laughing before she knocked on the door.

Troy was the one to open it, and he smiled broadly when he saw her. "Liza! What a surprise. Erica, babe! Your sister's here." He let her inside.

Erica came out of the kitchen, bits of flour splattered on her dark T-shirt. She gave Troy a kiss, and then he apologized to Liza but said he had to get to his shift at work.

Then Liza and Erica were alone.

The apartment was small, but very neat. Erica hadn't always been good at keeping things clean, but maybe she'd changed. Or maybe Troy was tidy. Her sister looked just as good as the apartment did. Her expression was happy, there were no dark bags under her eyes, which meant she'd been sleeping. And she sighed in adoration when Troy kissed her.

Liza had never seen Erica look like this.

"This is a surprise!" said Erica. "Do you want some tea? It's a little early for beer."

Liza wasn't much of a drinker anyway. "Tea would be nice."

Erica already had some made, and they sat side-by-side on the small couch.

Before Liza could ask any questions, Erica launched into a story about how Troy had tried to pick her flowers after work one day and ended up getting his hands covered in poison ivy. Then she talked about what one of her friends from high school was doing at the local university.

She had a dozen little stories.

And at no point did she ask how Liza was doing.

Or about their father. But Liza could understand that.

"We're moving into Mr. Grady's old place next month," Erica was saying. "I think it will be great for when we have the baby."

"Baby!" Liza looked down at her sister's stomach, but there was no sign of any little invader.

"What?" Erica laughed, shaking her head. "No, I'm not pregnant yet. But we're trying."

Liza tried to process that, tried to make it okay in her mind. She couldn't. And she exploded. "You're nineteen! You've been dating this guy for like two months. You shouldn't be having a baby with him." A baby would trap Erica here forever. She would never get out.

But Erica didn't seem to be considering that.

"You always just see the negative. First off, Troy and I have been dating for six months. Almost seven. I love him. He loves me. He treats me like a princess. And we're getting married." She held out her hand, and Liza saw the small gold band on her finger with an even smaller diamond on it. "Why can't you just be happy for me for once instead of trampling all over my joy? You always do that."

Liza stared at her sister for several seconds, her mind going absolutely blank, unable to process what Erica was saying.

Then she did. Then she understood the thing that she had been spending the last months, ever since Erica moved out, refusing to process.

Her sister didn't need her.

Her sister didn't want her.

Her sister didn't see everything that Liza had done to keep her safe.

And maybe that was a good thing. Maybe that meant Erica had a real shot at happiness.

But her sister's blindness made her angry. "Did you even know I was gone?" Liza asked. "Were you worried?"

"Did you go somewhere? Where? I didn't realize you left. I did send you a text. Is that why you didn't respond?"

One freaking text message. Erica lived two miles down the road from their father, from where Liza had been living, and where Liza dropped off the face of the Earth. And instead of worrying, Erica had only sent one text message.

Liza stood and set her teacup on the coffee table. "Good luck with Troy," she said. "I want you to be happy." She even meant it. But if she stayed here any longer, she might scream. She could feel that flame she'd called up when the wild dragons attacked, that link that pulled her towards Flint.

She was angry, but she wasn't about to set her sister's house on fire. Still, it was better to go.

Erica protested as Liza left the small apartment. But there was nothing else to say.

She had spent a very long time existing for her sister, sacrificing her life and her own happiness to make sure she was safe.

But that wasn't needed anymore. Maybe one day she might actually be happy for her sister; the pain and anger might subside into something gentler.

She couldn't sacrifice herself on the fear that one day her sister might need a safe place to land. Erica got to make her own choices.

And Liza got to live her own life.

But she wasn't sure exactly what that entailed.

There was a small park just down the road from Erica's apartment, and Liza sat on a park bench and observed the dingy little pond that didn't have any ducks, but currently had two white plastic bags floating on top of it. Someone would need to clean that up.

Where was she supposed to go now? She had the gems from Flint hanging heavy in her pocket. She could go anywhere on earth. She could find a way to go to college. She could get a job that she actually wanted.

But she didn't want any of that. And when a large masculine figure, one already so familiar even if she'd only known him for a few days, sat beside her she had to bite back a smile.

"You didn't leave," she said.

"Not yet," Flint replied.

He held out a hand.

Liza took it.

13

Liza was gripped with a bit of apprehension as Flint's ship rocketed through the sky. Was she making a mistake? She was choosing Flint over her sister. Over her entire planet. She was giving up the one thing that had driven her forward her whole life. And she'd just given Erica crap about betting everything on a guy she'd known for a couple of months. What did it mean when Liza was running with a guy she'd known for days?

It didn't *feel* like the wrong choice.

That made it ten times scarier.

Flint gripped her hand tight. He'd barely let go in the hour since he found her, as if he wasn't quite sure she wouldn't disappear. "Where do you want to go?" he asked softly. His voice was laced with hope and excitement.

And longing.

She smiled, squeezing his hand tight. "I have no idea."

He grinned. "Do you trust me?"

"You freaking kidnapped me, I'm not sure you've earned that." She was laughing as she said it. Something had changed in the last few hours, something loosened in her soul and made her dream of the larger world—or galaxy—for the very first time.

She felt like she could fly. With a dragon by her side, maybe she could.

"I have an idea," said Flint. He fiddled with the controls, and the ship lurched forward as they flew off towards space.

"Where?" Liza didn't even know if she cared about the destination. She felt alive in a way she never had before.

"You'll see. It'll take a few hours yet; I can show you the entertainment system, if you want, something to pass the time." He gestured to the back of the cockpit as if he was about to lead them out.

Liza tugged on his hand. And then she led him to the couch behind them with a grin. "I can think of something better."

He captured her lips with a groan. She felt it vibrate deep in his chest as she pressed against him, urging him down. She straddled his legs and opened her mouth to his kisses, delighting in the feeling of his hands running down her sides. He stroked her thighs, his touch searing through her clothes.

Dragon powers or sex powers, she wasn't sure. At the moment, she didn't care. She just wanted him.

He tugged her even closer, cradling her against his hard chest. Liza reveled in the feeling of his strong body holding her tight. Here, she felt safe. She hadn't known she could feel that way with a man. It was heady. He made her feel bold, made her feel like she could finally discover herself without guilt and obligation hanging over her shoulder. She could want.

She wanted him.

Liza tugged Flint's shirt up and over his head. The man was beautiful, every inch of him made her mouth water. He was cut, his muscles defined, his chest covered in short dark hairs.

Liza leaned in to nibble on his collar bone.

Flint hissed, arching into her touch, his hands stroking her back. "Are you trying to kill me, human?"

She just smiled and kept teasing his skin, delighting in his reactions, in the sounds he made.

She ran her fingers down his belly, reaching for the hard length of his cock and sliding her palm over his pants.

He bucked into her touch, eyes blazing with dragon fire. "You should not tease me." He kissed her again, thrusting his tongue into her mouth as if he could consume her. His hands slid under her skirt and up the smooth skin of her thighs, tugging at her panties as his fingers drew closer to the aching wet heat between her legs.

"But it's so much fun." She squeezed him through the fabric, and he let out a groan.

Flint lifted her up, and suddenly she found herself sprawled across the couch as he knelt before her. He nudged her legs apart with his broad shoulders, and her breath caught, knowing what he was going to do. He peeled her panties down like they were nothing, and then he was pressing his mouth against her slick folds, licking her with his tongue as he gazed up at her with his dragon eyes.

She hadn't meant to go this far, had only thought she'd earned the kiss. She was learning that with her dragon, she was playing with fire.

In more ways than one.

She cried out when his tongue found her center, teasing her as he licked up and down her folds. His fingers toyed with the edge of her opening, rubbing against her, and making her squirm with pleasure.

She could lie like this forever, but Flint upped the intensity until she was practically shaking with the need to come. She begged for him to do something, anything.

And then he did more, the pleasure of the thing sending her hurtling over the edge while crying out his name.

She expected him to join her then, to push into her and find her own release. Instead, Flint pulled back. His lips were swollen, and he had a satisfied look in his eyes.

"Get some rest," he said, caressing her leg one last time. "We'll be there before you know it."

14

Flint took her to the far edge of a galaxy she couldn't name, a crown of stars twinkling outside the view port. They'd been traveling for several hours at that point, and her body was still feeling the aftershocks of the pleasure Flint's tongue had given her.

The man knew what he was doing.

But the spectacle in front of her was enchanting enough to take her mind off sex. The stars seemed to dance in the sky, and somehow, they appeared in a rainbow of colors that Liza had never imagined.

Flint stood beside her, not quite close enough to touch, but she could feel the heat emanating off of his body. "I come here to think sometimes." He nodded his head towards the star cluster. "It's called the Nueva Crown. The last king of Nueva owned most of the star system, and he destroyed his kingdom in an effort to get closer to these stars."

"That's kind of depressing." But she could almost understand taking a risk for something so gorgeous.

"Well, he was a really crappy king, so don't feel too bad."

They both burst out laughing.

"I've never brought anyone here before." He turned and met her gaze with a sparkle in his eyes. "But I thought you might like it."

"I do." She settled into a seat in front of the view port and watched the stars dance. Flint joined her. She snuggled against him, and he put his arm around her. They didn't talk for a long time, just stared out the window and admired the beauty of the universe in front of them. But it felt so right sitting there with him, and Liza wondered if maybe this was a good place to start again. She reached up to stroke Flint's cheek. "Thank you for bringing me here."

He captured her hand and brushed his lips against her fingertips. "I'll take you anywhere you want to go."

"This is good for now." She wanted to take the time to truly enjoy this, wrapped up in Flint's arms and watching stars that had devoured an ancient kingdom.

She fell asleep at some point and slept soundly, safe in her mate's arms.

———

The journey didn't end at the Nueva Crown. The next day, Flint had them moving again, insisting that they'd miss the festival if they waited another moment.

She wondered if he was taking her to his home planet, but when they landed, it was clear he wasn't related to the blue aliens that were rushing to and fro.

"Welcome to Makaan," said Flint. "Come on, we're just in time." He grabbed her hand and tugged her into the throng and down a narrow street.

It was chaos and noise, a crush of people as far as the eye could see. Most were dressed in brightly colored robes, and there were fireworks going off in the sky above them.

But everyone was headed in the same direction, and Liza found herself swept along through the streets until they stopped in front of a large pagoda in a circular courtyard. There was a stage in the center displaying four statues carved of iridescent stone, lit from underneath and shining in the bright sun.

"What is this?" asked Liza.

"The Festival of the Rising," Flint said. They were closer now, almost close enough to touch the statues. "These four were once gods on this planet, but the people rose up and slayed them, turned them to stone. Every year they celebrate the day." He leaned in close. "Legend has it, though, that one day a mighty demi-god will come and free the gods from the stone and lead to a reign of terror never before seen."

"Uh ... let's hope that doesn't happen while we're here." She shuddered.

Flint laughed. "It's been four thousand years; I think we're safe."

They moved forward in the crowd that was growing thicker and more excited, people screaming and singing in such a cacophony that her translator gave up trying to understand.

They followed the crowd into a large market where artisans had artwork on display, some showing the final battle with the old gods, others with scenes depicting the majesty of Makaan. It was overwhelming in the best way. "Are you trying to show me all the beauty the universe has to offer?" she asked.

Her mate actually blushed! "I thought you would appreciate it. If you want, we can—"

"I do. It's just ..." She had trouble putting it all into words. "Seeing the universe like this is making me think of all the things I never saw back on Earth, you know?"

"I think I know where we should go next, then," he said. "But first, you need to try these fritters at this stall down the way. They're possibly the best thing I've ever eaten in my life."

They went back to Earth, but not home.

He took her to the Grand Canyon. It was bigger than she'd expected, even if she'd seen it in movies. The sheer magnitude of it made her feel small, which was kind of crazy seeing as how she'd just been in outer freaking space and had a firsthand look at the vastness of the universe. But the canyon was more personal. It had been forged by time, by the same elements that had made her.

It was hers, in its own way.

They could have stayed in the spaceship with its

wonderful temperature control and comfortable beds, but when Flint pulled out the camping gear, Liza smiled. She wasn't much for camping, but this was a place that called for it.

They hiked along a trail, holding hands but not needing to talk, not here. It was enough to take in the view of the red rock and the deep gorge. Somehow, they didn't meet anyone else, even though the weather was perfect.

She sort of suspected they weren't supposed to be in this spot, so far away from anything, but she wasn't going to complain. Not when it was perfect.

As evening fell, they ate dinner cooked over an open fire, roasted marshmallows for dessert, and she curled up in Flint's arms and let him play with her hair.

God, she was so freaking happy.

"Is this where you want to stay?" Flint asked. There was something like melancholy in his voice. "You could, you know, find a house near here and enjoy this beauty always."

She sat up and fully looked at him. "What's wrong? Do you want to go on your way?"

He shook his head fiercely. "No. That's not it at all."

"Then what is it?"

"All I want in all of existence is to share the universe with you. I promised myself I wouldn't push, that I wouldn't ask so soon, but I can't keep it in anymore. The longer I wait, the more this feels like a lie. What do you need to stay with me? Anything in my power, it's yours. You already have my heart."

She searched his face, saw the hope and the desperation there, the longing. She felt it herself, down to her bones. Liza looked up at the unbelievably starry sky above, the Milky Way on display.

He had given her the stars.

"I don't need anything else." Then she kissed him.

15

Relief surged through Flint, quickly overwhelmed by the taste of his mate.

His.

Truly his. For good.

Her arms were strong and sure as they wound around his neck, and her body just as he remembered, soft and giving under his caress. He gripped her tight and rolled them over so that he was pinning her to the soft ground, his hard body pressed against hers from head to toe. When they broke apart for air, he couldn't stop smiling. He had her now, and he was going to show her exactly what that meant.

Flint trailed hot kisses down her neck, delighting in the shiver that passed through her body. She was so responsive. It fed the hunger pulsing in his belly, matched the desire burning through his veins like wildfire. His mate. His to claim, his to keep.

His to pleasure.

"I want your cries to echo across the canyon tonight," he whispered in her ear. "Give yourself to me."

He could smell her desire in the air, and his dragon roared in approval. Her passion for him was a gift he could never fully repay, and it filled the space between him, fueling his dragon's fire. He would spend his days and nights trying his best to be worthy of her.

Starting now.

He nipped her shoulder through her shirt, and she gasped, clutching his hips.

"I'm going to make you mine," he said.

She leaned into him, offering herself up. "I've been yours for awhile now, dragon."

Her admission sent his blood racing. He stripped off his clothes, letting them fall carelessly to the ground. When he was bare to the cool air, he began to pull her garments off. There was no hurry, but his eager cock ached for attention.

First, he needed to taste. To lick every inch of his mate's warm, soft skin.

When she was bare before him, her breathing shallow and her pupils dilated with desire, he gently pushed her knees apart, kneeling between them as he gazed down at her gorgeous form. His for the taking. He slid his palms up her inner thighs, keeping her still when she squirmed beneath his touch, and he grinned. "I will always keep you safe, Liza," he growled, letting passion fill his voice. "You can trust me."

"I do." Her expression was vulnerable but there was a smile on her lips. She didn't look away. "I do."

He dipped his head down between her legs and teased his tongue over her core. She was wet, dripping already, and the smell of her made him wild. He growled, dragging his tongue over her slick folds and capturing her taste in his mouth.

Liza cried out and bucked up against him, but he kept her pinned with one hand on her thigh. With another flick of his tongue, she was trembling beneath his touch, gasping and moaning. He wanted to make her cry out even louder, to shatter under the power of his thrusts. It wasn't enough. He wanted more.

He wanted everything.

She was close. So open to him.

He devoured her, pushing her closer to the edge of ecstasy but pulling back before she tumbled over, gentling his strokes as she moaned in protest. He wanted to draw it out, to make her beg.

Then he wanted her unleashed on him and making him pay back every moment of sensual torment.

So, he kept teasing her, tasting her, driving her to the brink but not beyond. Not until she was begging him for more. Then he speared his tongue into her, pressing against her sweet spot and pushing her over the edge of her climax. He pushed her until she was a writhing mess, until she screamed out into the night sky, rebounding into the valley below.

Male satisfaction coursed through his veins. She was his. A groan of pure hunger and triumph tore up Flint's throat.

His woman.

His mate.

His forever.

And if he didn't get inside of her in the next minutes, he might actually go mad.

Flint guided his aching cock to her opening, then slowly, tortuously pushed inside.

It was agony and heaven in the same stroke. She was tight and wet, and she took him perfectly. Her body was made to be his, to welcome him home. He shuddered once he was all the way inside, fighting the urge to spill himself right there. But he was a dragon, and he had to prove his honor to his mate.

He moved inside of her, slow at first, then faster, increasing the pace as she rocked her hips against him. Her nails bit into his shoulders, scoring marks that burned with exquisite pleasure.

She clung to him. Her forehead pressed against his neck as a gasp tore from her throat and echoed out into the night sky. He felt her nails dig into his back as their bodies moved as one. Flint poured every ounce of devotion and love into the way he took her, needing her to feel it in every cell of her body. It was hard to remember anything in the galaxy except for this woman in his arms, giving herself to him with everything she had.

To know how cherished she was. How she was the treasure in his arms, worth more than a hoard of the rarest gems. She was his mate, and she was his whole world.

When her pleasure crested and she clenched around him, he finally allowed his own release, shuddering with the force of it. Flint claimed Liza's lips with a kiss as they collapsed in each other's arms.

He stroked her sweat-soaked skin, soothing her through the aftershocks of pleasure.

And he hoped that each of their tomorrows outshone today.

EPILOGUE

ONE MONTH Later

"Stop freaking out," Flint told her, as if that was something he had any control over.

"I'm not freaking out," Liza protested, rearranging the skirts of her ridiculous dress and hoping she wasn't about to embarrass her mate in front of his family.

And the king.

What the hell?

Though, luckily, she wouldn't have to deal with *that* potential train wreck until Flint's cousin's wedding in a week. Liza was just going to do her best to pretend it wasn't happening and power through.

In the past month, Flint had taken her to a handful of his favorite haunts, from the proving grounds of Polaris to the Celestial Speed Races on Kolterra Prime. But when he had gotten an invitation to his cousin's wedding on Vemion, he'd been so excited that she couldn't say no when he asked if she wanted to come.

She had to meet the in-laws sometime. She just really hoped his parents liked her.

"It's going to be great." Flint had the kind of confidence that only came from being completely solid in the knowledge that his family loved him and accepted him completely.

Asshole.

"I probably shouldn't mention the part where you kidnapped me, right?" She worried at a piece of detailing on the bodice of her dress, running her finger over the decoration.

"Oh, you should definitely tell them. They'll love it." He placed his hands on either one of her shoulders and kissed her forehead. "Just like I love you. Now come on, you faced down an angry wild dragon, you can handle my mom."

Liza wasn't too sure about that. Were water dragons a possibility? Nereus and Samantha's cave was looking like a great option right about now. She would have bolted if Flint's grip wasn't holding her in place.

She wouldn't abandon her mate. But this could still go very, very badly.

She squeezed her eyes shut and nodded at her mate. "Let's go."

He took her hand with a soft laugh. "You look like you're about to face an executioner. Did you know that Knox's mate tried to rob him? And my mother accepted her with open arms and an invitation to loot her jewelry room. Father has been developing some kind of playacting game with Asher's mate. This will go well."

Instead of taking her outside, he lead her to the roof.

"What are we doing up here? I thought we were taking a carriage?" There was a bit of a tremor in her voice, the vestiges of fear refusing to completely go away.

Her mate grinned. "I thought we'd fly." And, in a blink, he turned into a brilliantly colored dragon all sprawled out on the roof of Knox's townhouse. "*Hop on,*" his words whispered in her mind.

She'd seen his dragon form. He loved to go flying in the mornings, and he'd even taken her once, just before they left the Grand Canyon, though she'd been convinced they'd be spotted by the military and shot down.

It wasn't that she didn't trust Flint, but dragons didn't exactly have seat belts. Her worries lasted only until Flint took off. Then the wonder of flight wiped them away. They were probably there, somewhere, but she was riding a freaking dragon! What was there to worry about?

Liza laughed into the wind. Her dragon responded with a joyous roar, and she pressed herself to him, leaning down low against his back to watch as the town raced by. He soared over the capital city of Vemion, making lazy loops around the towers and turrets.

She knew his parents' estate wasn't far, but Flint seemed to be in no hurry. He circled over the palace twice, then over the market district where music could be heard even from the sky. Finally, he turned, heading over rolling green hills that gave way to the estates of noble houses.

They landed in front of an estate that was bigger than her elementary school.

As Flint turned back into a man, Liza's anxiety came back.

But then two older adults, both of them bearing a striking resemblance to her mate, came out, all smiles. Flint gripped her hand, and Liza let the worries melt away. Flint's parents swept her up in their arms, and her own mouth pulled into a grin.

She'd have to figure this family thing out.

She had Flint now. She couldn't wait.

———

WANT JUST ONE MORE SCENE?

Get a free bonus scene featuring characters from this book delivered straight to your inbox!
Sign up now: https://katerudolph.net/index.php/flint-bonus-sign-up/

Thank you for reading Knox! The series continues with *Flint*.

Read now!: https://shop.katerudolph.net/products/flint

Ready to give audio a try? Get a free audiobook here!
https://katerudolph.net/index.php/free-audiobook

PREVIEW CRUX

Courtney Lamb's feet were heavy, and she had the headache to end all headaches. She curled into herself on one side, trying to scrunch up into a ball, but her feet dragged along the floor and noise echoed off the metal walls around her.

She was still wearing her roller skates.

How? She always took them off before leaving work. She couldn't exactly drive with wheels on her feet. And yet, as she turned over and pulled her legs in, they slipped on the cold metal floor.

Where was she? This wasn't the root beer stand she worked at, nor was it the creepy, decrepit steel barn that sat on the very edge of the restaurant property. She looked around, squinting in the dim light and trying to get her bearings.

It was industrial, but the room was small. Steel

walls. No windows. And a weird echo-y noise in the distance that might have been an air conditioner.

She didn't see a door.

Courtney scrambled to her knees before realizing she wasn't going to get far with roller skates on her feet. She shucked the skates off and wiggled her toes in her sweaty socks before tying the laces together. No matter what was going on, she didn't want to lose her skates.

They were expensive. And one of the few nice things she had left.

There was a shriek down the hall, or at least, Courtney assumed there was a hall, and she flinched.

What the hell was going on?

Had she been kidnapped? Was she being trafficked? She'd seen plenty of Facebook posts talking about the perils of being a woman in America, but most of it seemed like a bunch of bullshit. People didn't *actually* hide under cars to slit the Achilles tendons of the unsuspecting.

Right?

She ran a hand down the back of her leg, as if to assure herself that she was intact. Obviously she was. Other than the headache, she wasn't hurt.

She was just confused.

And in trouble.

She wanted to call for help, but a second scream from somewhere in the building made her throat freeze up. No, she didn't want to call attention to herself.

With her skate laces tied together, she was able to sling her skates over her shoulder and get to her feet. The room seemed even tinier when she was standing up. Was she a prisoner? Why?

Her mom was going to kill her when she found out.

Of course, Courtney hadn't spoken to her mother in months, and now was not the time to think about how this would impact her mother's career. She was in the middle of an abduction, she had to care about herself.

She stroked the top of her skate, half for comfort, half to remind herself that it was sturdy and could probably be used as some kind of weapon.

She was wearing the thick leggings and short sleeve red tunic that made up her work uniform, though her name badge must have fallen off some-where. That furthered Courtney's theory that she'd been taken from work.

She couldn't remember clocking out. She wracked her brain, but the last thing she remembered was telling her co-worker, Sarah, that she didn't have any plans for the weekend. The same as every weekend these days.

That wasn't what she should be feeling bad about at the moment.

Was Sarah a trafficker? Had she waited to strike until Courtney was at her most vulnerable?

No. That was ridiculous. Sarah was a college student trying to make ends meet. She wasn't sinister.

Where was the freaking door?

Courtney whirled around, but she still didn't see anything that looked like it would let her out of the room. She was in a metal tomb and she couldn't escape.

Her breaths came faster and faster, and black spots danced in front of her eyes.

No. No. Now was not the time for a panic attack.

She hadn't had one in months, and she didn't want them to restart. They sucked.

And so did her whole situation.

"Think of the good things," she commanded herself. There weren't many. But she had to number them off. "I'm in my regular clothes. My skates are fine. I'm not hurt." She ran out of optimism after that. Any other "good" news sounded like asking for trouble, and Courtney wasn't interested in that.

She ran her hands over the metal walls, looking for a seam that might reveal a hidden door. There had to be something. She had been put in the room, so there had to be a way to get her out of it. She looked up, wondering if she'd somehow been lowered in, but the ceiling was too high to make out any fine detail in the dim light.

Where was the light even coming from?

There wasn't a ceiling light. She didn't see lights in the floor. There was just a faint, pale blue glow all around her that allowed her to see.

It was another good thing, and Courtney decided not to question it.

She had her skates, but she wished she had a skate tool. That fancy little wrench might have helped her pry an invisible door open. But her skate tool and spare wheels were in her bag at work. Along with her cell phone, a bit of cash, and her car keys. She had no way to contact anyone for help.

And *there* was the hyperventilation.

She tried to control her breathing, but the walls felt like they were closing in. She heard footsteps coming her way and shrank back as far away from the sound as she could. The room was maybe six feet wide. She couldn't shrink back much.

A brave woman would have done something. Courtney *wished* she was brave. But she couldn't think and she wanted to live. She was pretty sure brave people died quicker than cowards.

The wall opposite her glowed a faint yellow, and a rectangle formed before sliding to one side, the invisible door revealing itself. A brave woman would have charged.

Instead, Courtney watched a monster step inside.

It—and it was clearly an *it*, not a person—was some kind of *creature*. Over eight feet tall, antennae coming out of its head, and sinister purple skin that was covered in a faint slime. It wore clothes over most of its body, but its arms were exposed, and scars or tattoos or something covered it.

One of its hands wasn't a hand at all. Instead, it came to a fine point and had an edge that made it look like a sword.

It looked like something out of *Star Trek*.

And she was wearing a red shirt.

Shit.

It wore pants, but judging by the giant bulge right where his dick should be, he didn't plan on wearing them for long. And she didn't want to find out if his dick was a knife too.

Working by instinct, not pausing to think, Courtney grabbed onto one of her skates and swung, sending the other one flying at the monster's head. He didn't expect it, and the wheels, metal plate, and carbon fiber boot were enough to send him slumping to the ground.

Oh god, was he dead? Had she broken her skate?

Courtney flailed for a moment and cut off the horrible noise that tried to escape her throat. She checked her skate first. Except for a bit of slime and something that might have been monster blood, it seemed fine.

Good.

She didn't know how to check for a pulse on a monster. She didn't know if she wanted him to be dead or alive.

Oh god. What was she going to do?

She had to run.

She stepped around the monster and dove through the door, just in case it tried to close. The hallway was narrow and lit up by the same ambient blue light as her cell. She chose a direction and ran, unsure if it was correct but refusing to hesitate.

She stumbled when she passed a window.

Courtney came to a halt and looked outside.

She expected a city. Maybe some trees. *Something*.

Instead, she saw the black of space.

Outer space.

She wasn't in a warehouse. She was on a space ship, and they were hovering above some planet that didn't look like Earth.

How was she going to get home?

She was trying to think, then something impacted the ship, and Courtney stumbled as the lights went out and all of her senses went haywire.

JOIN THE CELESTIAL HEARTS CLUB

HEY THERE, **wonderful reader! Are you ready to take our relationship to the next level?**

By becoming a member of the Celestial Hearts Club, you'll get access to:

- early access to chapters from books before they're published
- exclusive short stories - at least one a month!
- sneak peeks that will make your heart skip a beat

Plus, you'll be directly contributing to the creation of more epic love stories and heart pounding space adventures.

Are you ready to hop on board and support the creation of more out-of-this-world romance?

Check it out!

https://katerudolph.net/celestialheartsclub

INTERGALACTIC DATING AGENCY

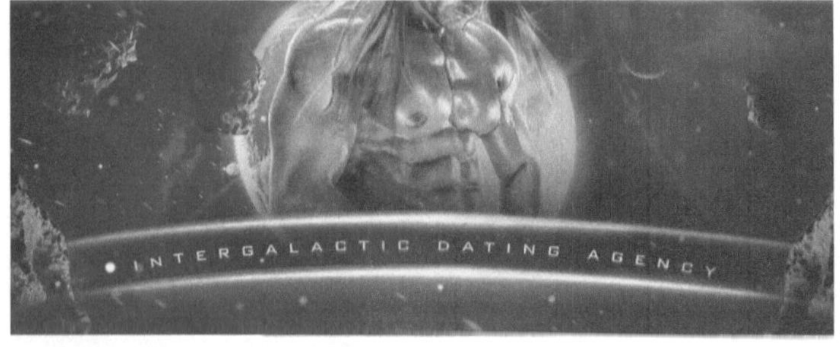

LOOKING for love that's out of this world? These strong, smart, sexy aliens are seeking mates from the Milky Way. Just hop onboard with your local Intergalactic Dating Agency. Join our group of authors as we explore the friendly skies and beyond with trilogies of cosmic craving, astral adventure, and otherworldly lovers. Warning: abductions may or may not be included!

ALSO BY KATE RUDOLPH

Dragon Brides

Dragon Princes. Fierce Women. Love.

Fated mates, fierce women, and dragon princes are ready to find their mates.

Crux

Ranger

Saber

Cipher

Storm

Drake

Asher

Knox

Flint

Guarded by the Shifter

Werewolf. Bodyguard. Mate.
The origins of these shifters are shrouded in
mystery, but they're determined to protect their
mates from any harm that comes their way.
Also available in audio!
Hunting Season
On the Prowl
Stalking Magic
Hungry for the Wolf
Wolf Cursed (novella)
Wolf's Temptation

––––––––––

Stealing the Alpha

**The thief takes what she wants, but the alpha
keeps what's his...**
Join shifter thief Mel as she clashes with lion alpha
Luke in an explosive trilogy of two opposites who
can't keep away from one another.
Also available in audio!
The Alpha Heist

Entangled with the Thief
In the Alpha's Bed

———

Alien Mates: Planet Exile

Guerran is no place for pretty human women. But these alien heroes will protect their mates!
Also available in audio!

Exile's Hunter
Exile's Adored

———

Zulir Warrior Mates

Kidnapped humans. Alien Warriors. Electric wings.
The Zulir Warrior Mates series brings you human heroines and heroes abducted from Earth who find love – and wings! – with the alien warriors who rescue them.
Also available in audio!

Synnr's Saint

Synnr's Hope

Synnr's Spark

Synnr's Kiss

Synnr's Ride

Mated to the Alien

Fated Mate Alien Romance

Detyens are doomed to die young if they don't find their fated mates.

Follow along as these mated pairs fight off aliens, corrupt dictators, prejudiced humans, pirates, and more! The books can be read or listened to in any order, though some characters show up in multiple stories.

Select books available in audio.

Pick a book and jump into the action today!

Ruwen

Tyral

Stoan

Cyborg

Krayter

Kayleb

Shayn

Braxtyn

Doryan

Dekon

Detyen Warriors

Detya was destroyed a hundred years ago. These doomed warriors are out to find justice... and their mates.

The Detyen Warriors series brings you kick butt heroines, alpha alien heroes, fated mates, and relationships strong enough to span the galaxy!

The entire series is also available in audio!

Soulless

Ruthless

Heartless

Faultless

Endless

Alien Holiday Romance

Christmas... in space????
These alien holiday romances look beyond Earth's winter holidays and ring in the season across the galaxy!
Select titles available in audio.
Snowed in with the Alien Beast
The Alien's Winter Gift
The Alien Reindeer's Wild Ride
Trapped with her Alien Mate

Alien Outlaws

Outlaws, schemes, and love... it's all there in the Alien Outlaws series...
Andie Munster is sick of life on Ixilta, the planet she got dumped on after being abducted from Earth six years ago. And when the mysterious and dangerous Xandr shows up looking for a way off the planet, she's half-prisoner, half-co-conspirator in a wild rush to escape.
Rogue Alien's Escape
Rogue Alien's Woman
Rogue Alien's Secret
Rogue Alien's Legacy

——————

Find more by Kate Rudolph at www.
katerudolph.net

ABOUT KATE RUDOLPH

KATE RUDOLPH IS a paranormal and sci-fi romance writer who lives in Indiana. She loves writing about kick butt heroines and the steamy heroes who love them. She's been devouring romance novels since she was too young to be reading them and had to hide her books so no one would take them away. She couldn't imagine a better job in this world than writing romances and sharing them with her fellow readers.

If you enjoyed this story, please consider leaving a review.

www.ingramcontent.com/pod-product-compliance
Lightning Source LLC
Chambersburg PA
CBHW031417200726
48285CB00017BA/2421